SEAGL...
&
other poems and stories

An Anthology by North Devon Writers

edited by

**Rebecca Alexander
& Ruth Downie**

Reb Alxand

Colin Z Smith

Cover art by Laughing Gull Design

SEAGLASS AND OTHER POEMS AND STORIES

Published by the North Devon Publishing Project

Copyright belongs to the writers named. The authors assert their rights to be identified as the author of their work(s) under the Copyright, Designs and Patents Acts 1988.

First published in Great Britain in 2015

ISBN 978-1-326-22901-6

ACKNOWLEDGEMENTS

This was a group effort, and I have a list of people to thank. But really, there is a whole community of writers who have supported this project by being writers, readers, who have critiqued, advised and encouraged the writers represented here. But to single out a sample of individuals to offer my gratitude to:

Jude Jeal, of Barnstaple library, who supported the idea of writing groups in North Devon,

Gillian Kerr, who took up the idea and let it blossom into the many writing related activities based in north Devon today,

Colin and Sue Smith for their ordering the collection, it was a mammoth task,

Colin Smith for his incredible work editing the whole book,

Vicky at Laughing Gull Designs, who created and designed the beautiful cover,

And the expert eye of Ruth Downie, an experienced author, who helped me with the difficult job of deciding what to put in (and what, with great regret, to leave out).

And most importantly, to all the writers who wrote, edited and polished up their poems and stories, memoirs and even a song, to make the charming and varied collection we have created.

FOREWORD

by Rebecca Alexander

My publishing career was launched by a competition. Having a target to aim for, and knowing that editors will choose the best of the entries makes writers work hard to be included. And pushing writing that little bit more gets the author noticed. Both Ruth Downie and I have benefited from competition and gained commercial publishing contracts, so introducing a competition in 2014 to offer writers in North Devon the opportunity to submit poems, fiction in all genres, creative non-fictions and songs was, for me, giving a little back.

In fact, I think I got even more back. I enjoyed reading all the submissions, some of them several times. It was hard to take out a short story, a piece of flash fiction or a story, very often because they were too similar to another entry or just a bit rough around the edges.

The few pieces of memoir here are very strong, beautifully written and atmospheric. Flash fictions, too, have impressed, not least because they have to work so hard to get a whole story into a tiny space, making words do several jobs at once.

Poetry is much harder to judge. There are some lovely stories told in poem form, some lovely haiku, even a few limericks for light relief. In the end, I included the poems I liked the most, I'm afraid, being ill qualified to judge their poetic merit!

The novel openings are intriguing, as a reader I could sense the whole story stretching out in possible strands, like a frayed rope. That's what a first chapter should do. I hope to read the finished books one day.

The short stories are delightful, some of them filled with pathos or dark doings, some funny, some evoking our beautiful countryside or the sea. They vary across the whole spectrum of humour, fantasy, science fiction, historical, romantic, contemporary suspense, crime and even retelling of a parable. They amuse, entertain and shock in equal measure.

I hope you enjoy the book, savour, test out the stories, read the poetry aloud, sing along with the song, make up endings for the novel openings, let your memories be stirred by the memoirs.

We writers only do half the work, pinning the outpourings of imagination onto the page in carefully chosen words. It's the readers that unravel, recreate and add their own imagination...

CONTENTS

Daddy's Coming Home	Pamela Kaye	11
Flutter	Rachel Carter	13
Sarah's Adventures of Matilda	Rebecca Alexander	15
Of Mice and Fire	Ruth Downie	16
Windmills in Andalusia	Gillian Kerr	19
It's An Ill Wind	Nora Bendle	20
The Wisdom of Solomon	Colin Z Smith	24
The Bone-Smile	Ben Blake	28
Hills of Green	Mike Rigby	31
A Nomad Child	Chris Hodgson	32
George and Alfred	Sue Somerville	33
Strike	Michelle Woollacott	36
Poet	Rosemary Alves-Veira	41
Kagome Kagome	Aidan James	42
I'll Tell you No Lies	Tori Jeffs	48
We Are What We Are	Sherrall Davey	51
Unfinished Painting by 'Canvas'	Helen Robinson	52
We Are a Grandmother	Pamela Kaye	54
The Longings of Habbib	Gillian Kerr	56
The Pianist	Susan Smith	61
My Grandmother's Kitchen	Anne Beer	64
Dragons	Rachel Carter	66
I'm Not Doing This Job No More	Russell Bave	69
Confetti	Helen Robinson	70

Earth Posthumous	Carey Bave	71
Antony's Colossus	Chris Hodgson	76
Love Song	Rosemary Alves-Veira	79
Seaglass	Rebecca Alexander	80
Valentine's Night	Colin Z Smith	81
Desert Island Discs from Hell	Pamela Kaye	84
Rags to Ringlets	Maxine Bracher	89
Growing Pains	Sue Somerville	91
Hello	Rosemary Alves-Veira	95
Wolves	Rosemary Alves-Veira	95
Viking Funeral	Rebecca Alexander	95
The Black Swan	Iain Shillito	101
First Flight	Angie Robbins	105
Night	Angie Robbins	105
Remembering	Angie Robbins	105
Spring Wind	Angie Robbins	105
Black Lord of Eagles	Ben Blake	106
Butterfly Dances	Colin Z Smith	109
Reflection	Sherrall Davey	112
Family Ties	Jessica McKinty	113
Going...Going...Gone	Rosemary Alves-Veira	117
Adam from Eden	Pat Fricker	122
The Lady from Pinner	Pat Fricker	122
The Queen	Pat Fricker	122
Golden Days on Exmoor	Anne Beer	123
Displaced	Gillian Kerr	125

Fat and Lazy Duck	Colin Z Smith	127
In Her Shoes	Nora Bendle	130
Country lanes	Sue Smith	133
The Swimming Pool	Diana Eilbeck	135
Harry	Colin Smith	139
Criteria	Rachel Carter	143
Epistle from Headmaster	Helen Robinson	143
Whose Fault?	Nora Bendle	147
Music Lesson	Helen Robinson	151
Things Ancient and Modern	Susanna Eccleston	153
The Foot	Rachel Carter	156
Co-creator	Rosemary Alves-Veira	159
Fox Rabbit Goose	Rebecca Alexander	160
Our Late Friend	Rosemary Alves-Veira	165
Contributors' Biographies		166

Daddy's Coming Home
Pamela Kaye

The house smells of carbolic and lavender from all the scrubbing and polishing. All day William's mum has been cleaning and tidying and still she bustles around the gleaming house, gilding the lily, as Grandma would say. It is a testament to how special a day this is that she is wearing her Sunday best, a dark green dress with tiny flowers all over it, and that her hair is wavy from the uncomfortable-looking curlers she wore to bed last night. He catches her pinching her cheeks and smoothing her eyebrows with a licked finger as she pauses by the mirror over the mantelpiece. Her face colours when she sees him looking and she briskly sets to with the duster again. For once he sits motionless while it is she who can't keep still.

'Cheer up. Daddy's coming home today.'

Trying to conjure up an image of his father he recalls the smell of tobacco and hair oil as he sits on those broad shoulders, his head almost touching the ceiling, remembers a hand ruffling his hair and the jaunty whistling of a popular tune. But not what he looks like, he can manage only a shadowy figure, a stranger.

He has seen other dads come home, some horribly injured, with missing limbs or faces disfigured by jagged scars, Robert's dad shaking and mumbling and said to scream at night. Worse than any of this, though, are those who return with dead eyes, as if their bodies have come home empty, leaving the dads behind on the battlefields.

The war is over. He knows he should be glad, but can barely remember life without it. The war inhabits the games that he plays with his friends, all guns and explosions, battles and bravery. At home, his lead soldiers are his companions through the long evenings with his mum as she knits or darns socks while he plays. At bedtime he packs up his army, and he and his mum drink cocoa together in the orange glow of the fire. She sometimes has a faraway look and he knows that she is thinking of his dad, alone in his muddy trench under the stars.

A sound startles him out of his reverie, someone is whistling. Then Mum throws open the door and is running. He sees the distant shape. Soon it merges with that of his mother. The boy can't move. He waits, head down, sensing rather than seeing the two figures moving hand in hand towards him.

'Hello William.'

He forces himself to look up at the speaker. He looks tired and his face is rather grey. Reluctantly the boy's eyes are drawn to those of the man. They are blue like his own and, like his own, his dad's eyes are not dead, but twinkling and brimming with tears.

Flutter
Rachel Carter

It was the flit of the butterfly's wings that changed everything.
When she saw it, perched perfectly still on a nettle, it was dark – like her.
She liked that.
Quiet and dark.
And alone.
Folded up against the world.
She drew her elbows into her sides and watched its antennae twitch. 'We're the same – you and me.'
But then it lowered its wings and she saw that she was wrong. It showed off its rich red-orange and its bright purple flashes and powder-blue-eyed stare.
In a multi-coloured flash it took off.
She watched the creature's papery flight lift and bounce and then disappear it; losing itself in a medley of yellow dots, orange silk hearts, green spikes, purple tongues and bright pink spears. Light petals fluttered, heavy pompom heads swung like upturned pendulums, and grasses waved. The colours altered as the wildflowers danced and bobbed in the sunlight. How inspiring nature was to have evolved a creature that adapted so cleverly to its habitat.
Sitting cross-legged and gazing out across the grasses and flowerheads, she tried to match long-unused names with remembered images: the red admiral, the tortoiseshell, the painted lady... but she didn't know what this one was. Butterfly spotting had remained in her childhood with so many other ephemeral memories.
She wanted to take a photo. One day she would take the perfect wildflower meadow photo: sky, flowers and one other element: a bee, a bird, a distant hill, a butterfly perhaps...
One day...
She looked down at the unopened corner-shop-vodka, with the wonky label, hammocked in the lap of her long summer skirt and

squeezed the pills in her fist until her palm begged to be relieved of the pain. Then she stood up – letting the bottle drop to the ground – and walked back to the hospital, shaking out the pills like seeds along the path.

They'd said his eyelids had fluttered.

There was still hope.

Sarah's Adventures of Matilda
Rebecca Alexander

We lie on candlewick, smell dust
and bedtime, run fingers down wiggly lanes,
pick loose threads, and tell each other stories.
Sarah's adventures of Matilda.

She maps out the island heaven
on the round of her knee,
tracing lines of flowers
in the story of her dress.

The garden destroyer invades,
crabbed and clawed, its fingers
bunching and creasing,
tearing away the layers.

The garden restorer plants bulbs,
smooths bedding, replaces chaos,
replants garish blooms, buries
the bodies in polyester.

And we laugh, rolling on the beds
until our stomachs hurt,
we snatch at breath
and tears spit down our cheeks.

Of Mice and Fire
Ruth Downie

The mice had the place to themselves for years, and what with the damp and the way that all the floors leaned on one corner of the foundations, they might have expected to stay until it fell down around them. But those were the days when any congregation that hoped to attract a minister needed to offer a house. For a family man fresh from a theological college and a one-room flat in Battersea, that spacious rural offering in Georgian brick must have seemed a palace.

My parents and I arrived in 1962, swiftly followed by the coldest winter of the twentieth century. People remember it as the year the sea froze. I remember it as the winter when I lifted the sheet to get in beside my hot-water bottle and met a mouse that had found a warm place to die. I can't remember where I slept that night, but it wasn't in the mouse bed. I was still an only child back then: there were other bedrooms where I could be sent to fasten my bedsocked feet around the warm bottle while my breath steamed above the blankets and the vapour drew icy patterns inside the windows overnight.

It was the winter of earnest discussions between my parents about the state of the kitchen Rayburn. My only job was to keep out of the way, but it was clear that the Rayburn was easily displeased. If it were not fed correctly and pampered in complicated ways that no-one fully understood, it would abandon us and leave us to freeze.

On evenings and Sundays a coal fire was lit in the lounge, a room whose name stemmed less from any possibility of comfort than from its contents: a television, a brown three-piece suite, a china cabinet and a piano. (The lounge was next to the dining room, so named because that was where the dining table had been abandoned to wait for spring.) Unless you were within six feet of the fire or it was Christmas, there were only two occasions on which the lounge felt warm. One was on first entering. The other was on exiting into the hall, where the chill that clamped around you reminded you of how lucky you'd just been back in there.

Venturing out to play with the neighbours was a reminder that we were lucky to have any sort of house at all. As we lumbered through the snow in our wellies it was only a matter of time before someone said, 'Are your toes dead yet?' If they weren't, we all hoped they soon would be. It was easier to concentrate on the finer points of building a snowman when the feet stopped sending urgent messages of panic, and went numb. We paid for it later, of course, with the maddening itch of chilblains.

The Rayburn staggered on until spring, fed with coke and twigs and cardboard boxes and sweet wrappers and old sermon drafts – rubbish burned not to save on landfill, but because coke was expensive and central heating an almost unimaginable luxury. Central heating was for people who had holidays in Spain and drank Martinis. I had only the vaguest idea of what a Martini might be, but it was part of a world that contained fast cars and girls with long legs and hair that didn't move. You could tell they had central heating because they wore dresses with boat necks and no sleeves. If you dressed like that in our house, you'd soon find yourself shivering under the blankets with two Disprin and the Vicks Vapouriser.

I only knew one person who had central heating. She was called Pat. When I admired her new bike she said I should tell my dad to buy one for me. I remember opening my mouth to answer and then deciding it was all too complicated. My memory may have invented the drinks cabinet in Pat's lounge but if it existed, I'm sure it was stocked with Martini.

Looking back across time and geography, I can see that we did indeed live in a palace. So many well-proportioned rooms, with their wide views over the long gravel drive and the vast garden. A Rayburn, long before they were fashionable. And all of it within twenty minutes' walk of the beach and commuting distance of London. With renovations that the church couldn't afford, some fashionably distressed furniture and the odd vase of dried flowers, we could have featured in 'Country Living'.

When I drove back down Mill Road for the first time in forty-five years, I steeled myself to knock on the door. I wanted to see what might have been: to find out who had made the church an offer it couldn't refuse, paid for the renovations, installed the fashionable furniture and the flowers, and invited their friends round for – well, probably not Martinis. But maybe a crisp glass of dry white.

Except I couldn't, because the house wasn't there. Vanished. Sunk back into the expanded gravel of what was now a church car park. I can only guess that the tilt had become too crazy: the dry rot had finally won, and now new generations of mice would be telling their children stories of a magical world that ended in disaster.

Our house has gone, but others have appeared. The puddles that once cracked under our boots have been smoothed over in tarmac. The derelict slaughterhouse where we weren't supposed to play lies under another building, and the spirits of the ponies I never quite learned to ride now munch on their ghostly hay in an exclusive development of executive homes called Stables Close.

I too now live in impossible luxury. But like the former vagrant with the just-in-case packet of biscuits under the bed, I know exactly where the hot water bottles are. I worry about power cuts, and the fact that we have nowhere to burn anything bigger than a candle. Because I was there when the sea froze, and a mouse crept into my bed to die.

Windmills in Andalusia
Gillian Kerr

Slender shafts of seeming marble
Rise tall from earth in classic grace,
Boldly stalk the Spanish landscape
Just as Spender's 'giant girls', *
The Pylons, trekked his English land.

Now, above these ivory pillars,
Gigantic sails smoothly turn,
Silent, endless, huge white petals
Never knowing native soil –
But with a beauty of their own?

To the man of La Mancha** windmills
Were 'hulking giants' with whirling arms,
And tried to slay them. Now, in England,
Men battle too against their mills,
But fight with words, not swords.

Spender's pylons, 'tall with prophecy',
Cervantes' windmills, 'so foul a brood',
Today, our turbines . . . the greed for power
To drive man's need goes on
Like the ever-turning cycle that powers the wind
That drives the sail.

* *The Pylons* by Stephen Spender (1909 1995)
** *Don Quixote, Man of La Mancha* by Miguel Cervantes (1547-1616)

It's An Ill Wind
Nora Bendle

Out of the blue the wind came with no warning. It had been warm and dry for several weeks. The earth was parched. Eyes of brazen daisies were wide open to the sun whilst the shyer pansies lowered their heads in need of shade.

Behind the row of solid semis their occupants worked, played or lazed in long gardens.

At number 1 the Benson boys, oblivious of the heat, hurled their fluorescent Frisbee. Their Yorkshire terrier rushed between them, barking furiously and leaping skywards in a fruitless attempt to purloin the disc.

In the greenhouse of number 2 Jack Mullins pinched out the side shoots of his tomatoes. The sun had brought them on a treat and Jack was looking forward to an early crop. He mopped his brow and frowned at the yapping of next door's terrier. Thank goodness Millie would soon bring him a cup of tea. He could see her filling the kettle at the kitchen sink.

In the garden of number 3 Matthew Channing in shorts, sweat glistening on his bare back, was edging his lawn after mowing the rough grass. He and his partner had not long moved in. The garden had gone wild in the worst sense and its recovery was slow and arduous. Matthew had asked Jack Mullins to reduce the height of his laurel so that more light would reach the Channing flower bed but Jack liked giving shrubs their head and didn't hold with newcomers wanting to alter the outline of his garden.

Alison Drew lay on the grass at number 4, her chin cupped in one hand whilst she wrote her tenth love letter to Shaun at number 5. The other nine attempts were screwed up beside her. Shaun didn't know she loved him. She would never post the letter. All the girls fancied him. Sometimes he said 'Hi!' when they reached their front gates at the same time and Alison would stumble up the path with jellied knees. She took a sip of coke and fantasised that Shaun had poured her champagne.

Her beloved, grudgingly weeding his father's vegetables on the other side of the fence, was totally unaware of Alison's dilemma. The heat was oppressive and Shaun on his hands and knees was not as imposing as when standing tall.

At number 6 the widow, Lizzie Henshaw, hung out her washing and went upstairs to make her bed. Lizzie was 58 and still working full time so there was little left over to care for her garden, let alone laze in it. Mike had been a passionate gardener and she hated letting it get out of hand. It seemed disloyal somehow. Lizzie couldn't cope. She could scarcely distinguish a flower from a weed. She wondered if she dare ask Mr. Carter, the retired bank manager next door, to help her, supply the expertise. From her bedroom window she could overlook his carefully tended patch. There were shrubs and trellises of roses, borders stocked full of colour and scent. A pond surrounded by pebbles and spiky things, a seat and arbour. Beyond the box hedge marched lines of vegetables. If she stood outside her back door on a calm night the scent from beyond the fence was as heady as the bouquets Mike grew her. Lizzie knew little about her neighbour. He seemed shy. Unmarried, he had lived with his mother until her death in the spring and now he lived alone. Sometimes on Saturdays she would see him unload his shopping by the garage and he would nod good morning to her. He never instigated a conversation. A pity really!

When Lizzie went upstairs to make the bed Adam Carter was sitting beside the pond, reading a newspaper and smoking his pipe. He put down the paper and reached for a tankard of Guinness beside him. He flicked out a drunken fly. He was lonely. He often wondered about Mrs. Henshaw next door. Perhaps she was lonely too. Adam had enjoyed exchanging tips and cuttings with her husband over the fence. He was sure that Mike would have been horrified to see his plot so neglected. He presumed that Mrs. Henshaw had no time to keep it in good shape. She just cut the grass occasionally. He considered offering to help, he would enjoy it, but didn't like to interfere. It wasn't his way. He sighed. Nice looking woman she was too!

21

There was a strange stillness in the gardens. The leaves began to turn up. They shuddered, and suddenly what appeared to be the start of a summer breeze became a full blow. The gust caught up leaves and dust.

At number 1 it dislodged a loose slate just as the terrier was racing past. The slate flattened the terrier and distracted the younger Benson boy who missed the Frisbee.

'Thank God that dog's stopped,' said Jack Mullins just before the Frisbee flew over the fence and, shunted by the gale, crashed through the greenhouse roof spilling his tea and slicing off six of his best Alicantes.

At number 3 Matthew Channing had just stood back to admire his edging when a loud crack announced the demise of a large portion of Jack's laurel, letting a considerable amount of light onto the Channing flower bed. True, the freshly planted lavenders were no longer standing but they could be replaced. Matthew was delighted.

Alison's love letter was snatched out of her hand and together with the nine crumpled ones landed at Shaun's feet. Shaun would soon know ten times over that Alison loved him.

From her bedroom window Lizzie Henshaw observed the domino effect from the top of the street of semis and watched with disbelief as two pairs of the Janet Reger silk knickers Mike had given her were ripped from the line and took the straightest route to Mr. Carter's arbour. One pair wrapped themselves around his pipe rendering him temporarily sightless and the other dropped into his tankard.

Lizzie clapped her hand over her mouth and withdrew from the window in horror. In her mirror she watched Mr. Carter disentangle himself, saw the look on his face as he realised what had smothered him. Holding them up he inspected the smouldering hole his pipe had made after his involuntary gasp. He then bent to retrieve the wet article. It looked no bigger than a handkerchief when he squeezed out the Guinness.

When the doorbell rang Lizzie thought she wouldn't answer. It rang again, and again. He must know she was in! Oh well! she thought, what the hell! Perhaps the beer swilled ones were retrievable. She opened the door, smiled.

He stammered... 'So...so...sorry...! These...this...came over the fence.' He produced a folded Sainsbury carrier. Lizzie held out both hands to receive it.

'So kind!'

Adam was about to turn away.

'What a wind!' she said, and added, 'Would you like a cup of tea?'

'Well, thank you,' he said, 'I would.'

After two cups and a ginger biscuit he offered to help her with the garden. There was a twinkle in his eye. 'It's an ill wind,' he said.

'It is indeed!' she laughed.

The Wisdom of Solomon
(1 Kings 3:16-28)
Colin Z Smith

Hannah stood before the king, head bowed, praying: *O Lord, hear the petition of your servant. Give me victory in my hour of need.*

Glancing sideways, she could see the deliberate erectness of the woman beside her, could smell the new-wine fumes from two feet away. Miriam would have to try to make sure the king would not detect the scent himself. Perhaps there was hope in that.

The king spoke. 'What is this dispute? Which of you will tell me?'

Miriam jumped in first, and Hannah's heart leaped. Perhaps if the king detected her drunkenness he might rule against her straight away. 'Lord King,' the woman was saying in a wheedling tone, 'this woman here and me both live in the same house. While she was with me in the house I had a baby, a son. Then three days later this woman had a son as well. Then that night this woman lay on her baby and he died. So she got up in the middle of the night and swapped my son for hers – my beautiful, alive baby, laying her dead son on me instead. Then when I got up in the morning I found my son dead, and I was heart-broken. But then I looked more closely – and it wasn't my son at all, O King. And I looked across at her, and there she was, feeding my son. It's my son that's the live one O King – not hers!'

'N-no!' Hannah blurted out, before she could stop herself. 'It's not true, Lord King. It's my son who's alive, I did no such thing.'

Her rival had turned to face her while she was speaking. Now a sneer passed across the other woman's lips. 'Ah, listen to her. She knows he's mine. He even looks like me. Same hair, same eyes, same everything. He doesn't look a bit like her. Don't you listen to her my Lord. She stole my baby, and I want him back!'

'He's mine!' Hannah protested again, desperately. 'It's true he doesn't look like me, but he favours the father. Please let me keep him, Lord King. He is mine, honestly he is.'

Miriam laughed, a crazy, drunken shriek. 'Favours the father indeed! You don't even know which one of the customers you had nine months ago is the father. And what would you do with a baby anyway? Never even had one before, have you?'

'No,' Hannah moaned. She felt close to tears. 'That's why I need him so badly. At my age, he's my last chance. Without him I'll have nothing! Who will provide for me in my old age?'

Her rival sneered again. 'What do I care about your old age? He wouldn't even last that long in your hands. Wouldn't begin to know how to look after him, you wouldn't.'

Hannah was stung into a retort. 'What, like you, you mean! Look at the other two you once had. You treated them like slaves, and worse than slaves, young as they were. And then, when you'd used them up with fetching and carrying, and stealing for you, you sold them off for a loaf of bread and a pitcher of wine.'

'Garn,' her rival snarled. She was beginning to lose control, and her words were starting to slur – she didn't even appear to have noticed the accusation, or try to deny it. 'Least mine won't grow up to be no prissies like yours would. Learned to stand on their own two feet, mine did. Quick wits and a good bit of healthy discipline – that's all they needed.'

'Healthy discipline? You beat them till they were black and blue! I couldn't get to sleep some nights for their crying, and your cursing them. How could they have grown up to know love with you treating them like that?'

'Love!' the woman shrieked. 'Love! What's love got to do with anything? What man ever showed me love, lumbering me with two whining brats then clearing off and leaving me to a life of whoredom? Why should I show love to a couple of useless, clinging good-for-nothings, who ate the bread off my table and spat in my eye so much as look at me. And why should this new one be different? Why should I...'

The king, who'd been silent all through this exchange, suddenly roared, *'Enough!'* and Hannah jumped in astonishment, having forgotten all about him. As one, she and her rival turned to look at him. He was frowning deeply. 'Mistress Miriam,' he said, 'do I take it from what you have said that you wish to withdraw your claim to the child?'

There was a pause, and a complex interplay of emotions passed across Miriam's face while she appeared to be thinking about this. Then she glanced sideways, and Hannah saw hard-heartedness replace all other expressions. 'No, Lord King,' she said determinedly, 'I stick with what I say. The baby is mine – and I want him!'

The king frowned again, and seemed lost in thought. Then he looked up, and motioned for the baby to be brought to him. Hannah's heart plummeted, and at that dreadful moment she was sure that she had lost. It was true, there was a resemblance to Miriam in the child's looks, and none to her. The king couldn't fail to decide in the other woman's favour on that alone.

The king looked down at the child for a long moment, and then up again at the two women. Suddenly, he appeared to reach a decision. He spoke, and his words sent a chill of terror coursing through Hannah. 'Bring a sword,' he ordered one of his attendants standing by. 'Cut the child in two. Give one half to one woman, the other half to the other. They cannot be decided between – both shall gain what they desire.'

The world stopped, and silence filled the room. Then – 'No!' Hannah screamed. 'No! No! No! Give her the baby – her! Don't cut him in two! Don't – oh please don't!' She broke down sobbing.

'Ah,' Miriam was slurring, 'fair enough. I've just about had it with this rubbish. Cut the brat in two and let's have done with it! Neither of us'll have him.'

The king smiled, and the smile was not a friendly one. 'The matter is decided,' is growled. 'Let the woman Hannah have the child. Do not kill him – she is his mother. And as for you, Mistress Miriam...'

But Hannah had fainted, and did not hear the rest, or the fate of her rival. But when she returned home later that day, baby Josiah in hand, Miriam was not there, nor did she ever return again. And as she lay at night, the baby in her arms, Hannah would look over at the sleeping place where the other woman had lain, and remember the night she had sneaked over and laid a newly-dead baby in the other's arms, taking a living one in return – a living baby for her to love, and to provide for her in her old age.

The Bone-Smile
Ben Blake

It was past midnight when the man spoke. The hour when spirits walk, and wise men lock their doors.

'It's going to kill me,' he said. 'Isn't it?'

'Yes,' Kezia said.

'There's nothing I can do?'

'There is always something we can do,' she answered. 'But first we have to know what it is, or have time to learn it. You do not know, and your time has run out. I think you know this.'

'I'm going to die,' the man said. His tone held more wonder than it did fear, as though he'd never really believed until now that he was mortal. Many men did not. It wasn't a sin.

'It is *brigaki dulia* to us, a sorrow song,' Kezia said. 'We will lay out your body, my friend, and plug your nostrils with wax so evil spirits cannot enter in and possess you. We will give you dignity. But we cannot give you life. Not against this, and not yet.'

The man's head lifted. 'Yet?'

She hadn't meant to say that. Kezia's mouth tightened in irritation, an expression the man wouldn't see in the dark. But saying more did no harm, in the circumstances. 'There are suggestions that these creatures are not immortal. That they may be vulnerable.'

'You tell me this *now*?'

'The knowledge would not have helped you. It may be nothing in any case. Just leaves in the wind.'

'They're not creatures anyway,' the man said. 'There's no life in them, no heart or lungs or blood. Whatever moves them is as mechanical as a water wheel.'

It was much more than that. If a water wheel learned how to move as it chose, if it taught itself to hunt and kill, then the comparison would be more valid. Not wholly so, because some life had no need of heart or blood. Herbs were alive, and Thorn Cushions, and Weeping Apples. She didn't point that out. What good would it do now?

She tamped tobacco into her pipe and lit it, puffing blue smoke. It calmed her, a little. One could never be entirely at ease when one of those...*svatura* was near. Something unnatural, a being that lived yet did not. There was said to be a place in Time for everything, a space set aside for it alone. Kezia didn't think it was true of the *svatura*. Heresy, but it was what she believed.

'The world is remade instant by instant,' the man said. He had leaned back and was looking up at the sky, where clouds were drifting away eastwards and stars glimmered in their wake. A glowing edge of cumulus promised a sight of the moon soon enough. 'All of it, every grain of sand or drop of rain. But I won't be. I will be gone.'

'Everything dies,' she said gently. 'Everything except Time herself, who is infinite. In endless time, everything will one day come again.'

'But it won't be me.' He sounded plaintive now. 'I will never have another life. I end tonight.'

She could have comforted him. Told him what the *draba* believed – that something was approaching, something other than the monstrosity which stalked closer every moment. Change, perhaps, at least a chance of it. Or perhaps just another slaughter, one more culture smashed into splinters in the mud, but she wouldn't have to mention that.

The moon emerged from behind its cloud, and there was a figure standing in the meadow, cowled and robed.

Kezia's pipe had gone out. She made herself light it again, knowing the figure had no interest in her. It was *svatura* but that didn't make it clever. The thing had no brain of its own, just whatever impulse was given to it, and that urge was to hunt. It had tracked the man as he fled, following the line of his travel without pause or rest, until it ran him down in the valley below where the caravans were parked for the night. Where it would kill him.

The man stayed where he was, leaning back on his elbows, as the cowled figure started forward. 'Would you leave me, please?'

'If you wish,' she said, surprised.

'I do. I'd prefer you not to see this.' He glanced at her. 'Being close to one of these things can burn the flesh. And the memory. Go.'

She stood, smoothing her long skirt, and he added, 'Tell the others, if you can. Tell them what I tried, to escape this. At least the next poor fool will know it, for whatever good it will do.'

No good at all, probably. Nothing had ever worked against these robed killers. Not sword or spear, not crashing boulders or hoisting nets. Not even quintessence. They came and killed, and then were gone. It had been so for thousands of years.

She went as far as the line of trees and turned back. She didn't like leaving him alone, though she knew she was as helpless as he was. The cowled thing was only yards away now. She imagined she could feel the chill spreading from it, like *kuhr* frost on the high mountains. There was a plunge in her innards that made her think of death.

'May Kāla turn her many faces to smile on you,' she said. 'Go in peace, Maratos, and know you were loved.'

He turned to her, astonishment registering on his face that she knew his real name. His mouth opened, but then the Stalker was on him. A sleeve moved and Maratos fell back into the grass, mouth open, stars in his dead eyes.

Hills of Green
Mike Rigby

Oh, hills of green with stones of grey,
You never speak to me the way
you used.
Can you not whisper to me once more,
Those tales of adventure and of war,
Of which I was once such a part?
Have you lost your tongue through your ageing years?
Or is it I, the one who has aged the more,
Who has lost the ears?

A Nomad Child
Chris Hodgson

One of the women
The youngest, least pretty, most insolent
She rides like the wind
And shoots from the saddle
Every arrow straight to the mark

A nomad child
The faithful tribute of some minor tribe
Scarcely counted as one of the best
She's sweeter to me
Than eternal rest

By a river with a source unknown
I dismount
'My Lord, what is it?'
Nothing, a swooning desire
Just that, remount and ride away

But my nomad child, insolent always
She, so young and unafraid
Dares urge me on
'Lord, shall we seek?'

Follow that river with a source unknown
Stay faithful to a hopeless quest
'Let us go, you and I'
Search lands beyond eternal rest
And perish there.

George and Alfred
Sue Somerville

George surveyed the small lawn with a satisfied eye – yes, the stripes were perfect. He finished watering the pots and returned to the kitchen.

'The garden looks a real treat love, you should be pleased with it, though I'm sure the grass would have waited until you get back tomorrow,' smiled Doreen. 'Lunch is all ready. You OK for time?'

'Yes, fine thanks.' George washed his hands in the kitchen sink, straightening up the bottle of hand wash and smoothing out the towel before hanging it back on the rail. 'I'm taking the 4.30. I've booked a window seat with a table and my overnight bag is ready. So just a quick shower and change and I'm ready to go.'

He was looking quite dapper when he reappeared. Navy suit, pale blue striped shirt and darker spotted tie, gleaming shoes, hair neatly parted.

'You do look smart dear. Have a good time but don't overdo it. You boys can get carried away at these meetings.' Doreen checked him out and gave him an affectionate kiss on the cheek.

'Try not to!' laughed George. 'But it will be less stressful to stay the night, rather than rushing for that last train. It's always such a rush at the end and you're never sure of a taxi at that time of night. You don't mind do you love?'

'No. Really I think it's a good idea, and honestly I'm quite looking forward to an evening by myself.'

'Good girl. You have a nice time and I'll see you tomorrow. I haven't booked the train coming back, but it'll be mid-morning I should think. I might take a stroll along the Embankment after breakfast. Have a look at the old stomping ground.'

'Yes, why don't you? That would be nice. Off you go now.' Doreen waved from the doorway.

George set off towards the station, humming gently to himself, excitement mounting. He bought a copy of The Telegraph and settled himself in his seat. By the time he'd finished the crossword and folded the paper away the journey was three quarters over. He checked his watch. Alfred would be there by now.

George put his key in the door and stepped into the hallway. He stood for a moment absorbing the intoxicating perfumes... Coq au Vin, he made a guess. And what was it? Chanel? The soaring notes of Vaughan Williams' Lark Ascending filled the apartment. George gave a sigh of pleasure. The outside world receded, wounds soothed, his senses restored.

'I'll just be a minute!' Alfred shouted from the bathroom.

'Take your time – no hurry.' George poured a glass from the bottle of champagne, which was already chilled and waiting in the ice-bucket. He wandered into the kitchen and confirmed it was indeed Coq au Vin simmering gently on the stove. A peek in the fridge revealed a smoked salmon mousse with tarragon dressing and a pear and almond tart. Alfred had excelled himself.

He returned to the sitting room. The music had moved on. Debussy? There was no rush. He had planned what he was going to wear and he already had a good idea of the persona Alfred would adopt tonight. Vaughan Williams and Debussy indeed! But it was an interesting choice. Alfred was obviously going up-market. Last month George had been greeted by the smoky tones of Nina Simone, slow cooked pinto beans with chorizo and an underlying stingingly, spicy, exotic perfume, which thankfully he had never come across before.

'OK,' shouted Alfred. 'No peeping!'

George closed his eyes contentedly and waited for Alfred to disappear into his bedroom. He refilled his glass, ready for a soak in the bath before dressing. He selected his apparel, hanging it on the front of the wardrobe, and laid out all the toiletries and accoutrements which might be necessary to ensure his appearance would be perfect.

At seven o'clock precisely George opened his bedroom door and made his way to the sitting room.

'How do you do?' enquired Alfred, languidly extending a hand, the long red fingernails showing a diamond ring to advantage. 'I'm Margot – so pleased to meet you.'

'I'm Charlotte,' replied George. 'But people call me Charlie. I love your gown,' he smiled. 'Is it Dior?'

Strike
Michelle Woollacott

'That's it, Erin. Swim to me.' I stand a metre away from her in the pool, my arms outstretched. Her little white arms poke out of pink armbands as she grips the side with both hands. Her face is turned to me, her olive eyes calling.

'Just push away and I'll catch you.' My elbows are bent and if I were to stretch my arms, she could touch my rubber wristband.

Around us, children's laughter bounces off the ceiling. Waves of chlorine clean the air. Out of the window, trees bend and rain slams into the glass.

Water trickles down Erin's thin shoulders. She is growing out of her toddler fat.

Her face tells me she is not letting go of that edge.

Dan had always wanted children. As I cooked one autumn evening, he put his arms around my waist, as he often would, chin on my shoulder, and said, 'When are we gonna have a little one?'

'One day.' I kept my back to him. 'There's plenty of time.'

It had been dark for hours but the bare bulb kept our little kitchen bright. Dan brushed his stubble against my ear. 'Why don't we just... strike? We can take our little man to the park on Saturdays for a kick about.' He flicked an eyelash against my temple. 'I'll take him to see Barcelona—'

'What if we have a girl?' I laughed, adding noodles to the stir fry, 'and she likes, I dunno, netball, or swimming?'

'Girls can like football.' He pinched my waist.

'Can you get the plates?'

'Don't change the subject,' he grinned, but moved to the cupboard.

I stiffened. 'You can't shut yourself in the dark for hours if we have kids.'

He stopped. He forced the plates down onto the worktop. 'I'm feeling much better, thanks. I can't help it if I get headaches.'

'You could go to the doctor.' I tossed soy sauce into the pan.

'Doctor, shmoctor.'

The sizzling grew louder and I threw the food onto the plates. Grabbing glasses, he marched out of the kitchen.
'You need to sort it before we can think about that,' I smarted after him with the dishes.
Then came the smash.
Dan had fallen to the floor. His eyes were closed. A dark-red patch appeared from under his hairline.
Then came sirens, specialists, tests, scans.
I remember the speckled-grey wallpaper in the doctor's office, the heart-shaped shaving cut under the doctor's nose. The squeeze of Dan's hand in mine.
But most of what the doctor said as he sat across from us was a fuzz – apart from that one apologetic, stabbing sentence. 'You've got a few months...maybe six...'
My chair collapsed from under me. My skull ached and my coccyx stung.
The jagged Artex ceiling came into focus. I heard a far-off scream. It was coming from me.
At home, I lay my head on his lap, holding the warmth of his twenty-six year-old body. He sat, rigid.
Traffic whizzed outside; commuters eager to get home to their tea, to their TVs. To their children.
A crumpled tissue teetered on his jeans.
The evening grew dark but neither of us moved to turn on the light.
Finally, my breath was enough to blow the hankie off his knee. He whispered through the blackness. 'What are we...?' He looked down at me, far away and pleading.
I sat up and lodged my fingers into his fluffy hair. 'We're gonna...do everything we thought we had a lifetime to do. Starting with Barcelona.'
Our hotel room was as grand as we could afford and not far from the stadium.
'What was the ref thinking?' Dan was still ranting as we burst into the suite. 'I can't believe that goal was disallowed.'

I kissed him hard. 'That was to stop you talking about football all night.'
He pulled me close.
'Wait,' I scrambled for my bag and grabbed my full pill-packet.
He stared. 'You haven't been taking them?'
I strode across the room and dropped them into the bin. I stepped towards him, pushing him onto the bed.

Machines on unstable wheels held onto walls with their wires and leant on the bed with their tubes. Nurses glided past the door like passing traffic.
A shrunken man lay before me, his skin ashen, his cheeks hollow. He managed to raise a bony hand to gesture to the bedside cupboard.
I opened it and found a small gift-bag.
'For our little one,' he rasped, his grey eyes glistening. He took my hand and brought it to my stomach.
I lay beside him, curling in to his shrinking body.

Erin's legs kick frantically under the water as she remains gripped to the side.
'That's it!' I smile. 'Just push to me and I'll catch you!'
Determination fills her eyes. She reaches an arm towards me. Taking a deep breath, she kicks away from the wall and, in a second, she is in my arms.
'Well done!' I cry.
'I did it!' She bounces in the water. 'I'm a mermaid!'
'You are!' I hug her. 'Do you know what time it is, mermaid? It's time to take you home.'
Erin kneels on the plush carpet in her princess pyjamas with her dolls. Her freshly washed hair is combed behind her ears. All around us stand heavy-duty cardboard boxes but the room is void of furniture, of photos, of faces.
She hands me a curly-haired baby whose eyes close when you tip her back.

'I like playing mummies and babies.' I fiddle with the lace hem on the doll's dress. Veins protrude from my wrinkled hands. 'I tried to make a real baby once, a long time ago. But it didn't work.' I turn as a manicured young woman enters.

Madeline's expensive suit cuts her figure and her chocolatey hair falls over her shoulders.

I push a chlorine-scented strand from my face.

'Mummy, why can't Jennie come to Canada with us?'

Erin's mother sits on a box across from me.

'I'm sure you'll find a lovely new nanny in Canada,' I smile. 'So you're all packed?'

'Yes, I think so,' the child's mother smiles. 'Can't believe we're off tomorrow! What about you, Jennie? Have you...got something lined up?'

'Erm, no, no. I'm getting too old for this game. I've been nannying for forty years, you know. I'll...have my time,' I beam. We can hear the hard rain outside.

'Well...I should get Erin to bed...'

'Oh, of course. Come here, little one.' I squeeze her.

'Will we see you again?' the three-year-old asks.

Madeline pipes in: 'Oh, I'm sure we'll come home to visit.'

'Next time I see you, you'll be such a good swimmer, you'll have turned into a real mermaid,' I whisper, and Erin laughs.

'Don't forget your presents.'

I have to release Erin to take the gift-bag from Madeline. 'Thank you.'

'And thank you, for everything you've done for us these past three years.'

'Good luck!' I'm heading for the door, into the harsh night.

Erin waves from her mother's arms as I reach my battered old Beetle.

I wave back. And I leave.

The wind screams as I pull up at home. I wonder if my weathered car will stand the night. It was fit for the scrap heap years ago. Leaves hop along the pavement and bin-bags are strewn down the street. I look to my first-floor flat and the bedroom window is agape, the curtains flapping like sails. I am sure I closed that this morning.

I unlock the door and hobble upstairs. I dart into the bedroom. Papers are scattered across the floor and clothes have been blown from the top of the chest. I run to the window. The catch is stiff. I must not have closed it properly.

I drift into the kitchen and switch on the kettle before returning to the bedroom.

Setting the mug on the bedside table, I begin to retrieve letters and receipts from the floor. My eyes fall on the pillow. The shirt is gone.

I'm on my knees instantly, scrabbling among clothes and paperwork. I pull shoes, boxes and used tissues from under the bed.

The lights flicker and then they are gone. I feel around in the dark, the cruel night banging at the window.

Finally, it is there, hiding behind the bedpost. Suddenly I don't hear the outside frenzy anymore. I pull out the crumpled rag and a musty smell disbands. So old, yet new and unworn. Unfolding it, I strain my eyes to make out the baby-grow. On the front are a blue embroidered football and the words, 'Daddy's Little Striker'.

I perch on the bed in darkness, my knees stiff. I grasp the tiny piece of clothing to my stomach with cold fingers. I am still wearing my sopping coat and shoes. I stare past the fallen 'Happy Retirement' card and the unopened gift-bag on the floor.

And I let my tea go cold.

Poet
Rosemary Alves-Veira

What could be worse
Than a poet in the rain,
Howling in pain,
Words all a-scatter:
A shoal on the platter.

What could be worse?
(apart from this verse)

He dives to retrieve
From a tumbling tide
His slippery catch
Rearranged to match
With a scurrilous moon
On a windy night,
Birthing a star,
Or a terrible fright
In words that will chime
With the pain and the rain
In the eternal halls of his heart

Be kind to this soul
Wet footprints and all,
Should you find him
Lost and alone.
He doesn't ask much
When down on his luck
But don't feed
Or he'll follow you home.

Kagome Kagome
A James

かごめかごめ
Kagome kagome
籠の中の鳥は
Kago no naka no tori wa
いついつ出やる
Itsu itsu deyaru?
夜明けの晩に
Yoake no ban ni
鶴と亀が滑った
Tsuru to kame ga subetta.
後ろの正面だあれ
Ushiro no shoumen daare?

Kagome, kagome

The bird in the cage,

When, oh when will it come out?

In the night of dawn

The crane and turtle fell.

Who is behind you now?

'Good morning, my Princess,' the paper door slides open and a grizzled-looking man calls into the room.
'Mmmm-mmhhh.'
The man, clothed in sky-blue shitagi and hakama, emblazoned with red spider lilies, knee-walks into the room carrying a tray on which white rice steams. He beckons to two maids behind him, who follow and begin extracting clothes from behind sliding doors on either side of the room.
'You must wake, Kagome-himesama, for a princess must never be tardy in her duties.' He gently stirs the sleeping beauty awake, making sure to not grip too hard lest she break.
The princess rises from her slumber and as she sits up from her futon her long chestnut hair falls down behind her. She rubs her hazelnut eyes open and addresses the old samurai sitting next to her: 'Good morning, Amatsuda-san. What time is it?'
'It is eight o'clock, Princess. Your celebrations after agreeing to marry Jingoro-kun ran long, so I felt an extra hour's sleep would be acceptable,' Amatsuda responds in kind.

'Thank you, Amatsuda-san. Everyday I'm reminded why you were my father's most beloved friend.' She smiles at her premier retainer and readies herself for her morning routine.

'Excuse us, my lord.' The maids bow to Amatsuda and he excuses himself to stand guard outside.

The morning air is crisp and takes small icy nibbles from the Princess's face as she walks along the veranda. She flinches as a gust blows past.

'Is there a problem, Princess?' Amatsuda turns to face the young woman.

'This morning feels chillier than yesterday. Is winter upon us already?' Kagome ruffles her regal pink kimono in an attempt to warm up.

'I expect that winter will come soon, but it is unusually cold. As winter approaches so does the anniversary of your parents' deaths; do you wish to travel to your family grave?'

'Yes, of course. Not only to see them again, but I also wish to see more of what lies beyond these walls.'

'Princess?'

'I have spent so many years safe in these ancestral grounds that I wish to see the outside once more before I am wed. I wish to see the devastation I have heard in rumours about the wars outside and understand why our clan's land was so important that my parents were murdered.'

'Kagome-hime,' a contemplative voice calls to the pair from just ahead. As they turn they see a tall samurai wearing jet-black armour trimmed with crow feathers. 'I fear that such a trip will be dangerous even with all of us, your loyal retainers, at your side.'

'Hanataka-san. You were listening?' Kagome reluctantly questions the slender man in black.

'I overheard your desire for adventure. I cannot advocate questing on a whim given these explosive times. I'm sure Amatsuda-sama agrees,' Hanataka replies, pausing to compose himself.

'Indeed, I will have to agree with Hanataka-kun today, Princess. He may seem cold, but he worries for you as much as the rest of us.' Amatsuda glances at Hanataka, who simply bows his head in agreement. 'We shall discuss further with the others. Which reminds me, I heard Jingoro-kun's and Onigashima-san's voices quarrelling earlier: have you seen them, Hanataka-kun?'

'Those fools are making merry with the frost on their breath by the front porch. Shall we meet them there?' Hanataka scoffs at his colleagues.

'Yes, let us see them now.' Kagome beckons to be led forward.

The sounds of merriment from the front porch are the result of three more samurai: a broad man with impressive physique and hearty laugh in deep red armour; a leaner man in amber armour with six tassels lazily hanging from his back, who appears not much older than the princess; and an unremarkable warrior in white armour. The jovial two appear to be making fun of the plain-looking samurai.

'Speak up! Honda-san! If you do not! We cannot hear you!' the large samurai roars with laughter.

'Onigashima-san, I fear raising my voice as much as you may rip my throat apart,' the white samurai states, becoming more frustrated.

'I'm sorry, Honda-san, but even my clever ears couldn't hear that!' the young man taunts his peer.

'Onigashima-san, Honda-san and Jingoro-san. I'm glad to see you all in such high spirits,' Kagome makes herself known as she strolls towards the three merry samurai.

'You two make so much noise,' Hanataka scoffs at his allies as he leads the princess.

'Not you too, Hanataka-san,' Honda weeps, realising he's being ignored. 'Amatsuda-sama, Kagome-himesama, I have urgent news.' He redirects his attention to Kagome in an attempt to call reason. His statement is followed by commands from the other samurai to speak up, with Kagome's innocent laughter providing chorus.

'My lady, it's about Turtle Mask and Yamatsuru-sama,' Honda states, with more emergency.

'What about Turtle-san and Yamatsuru-san?' Kagome asks, detecting Honda's alarm.

'They're both dead.' Everyone falls silent. 'They were both murdered last night. By ninja, I assume from the kunai in Turtle Mask's back.'

'Those cowardly assassins!' Onigashima roars as loud as he can.

'How can that be? That old man has deflected sneak attacks from ninja before! I've seen it with my own eyes!' Jingoro states, bringing realisation to his elder peers.

'When I checked their bodies I found their throats slit and only Turtle Mask was hit by kunai.' Honda's comment causes the other samurai to murmur. 'Also...' His addition draws hushed attention. 'Their swords were stolen. *Only* their swords.'

The silence across the swordsmen and the princess draws long as they all contemplate the meaning of the theft. They are all fully aware that their swords are stamped with their family insignias, providing easy identification. There can only be few reasons an assailant would steal their weapon.

'Maybe they needed proof that their target had been killed,' Onigashima offers.

'Or maybe their weapon was stolen to implicate them in some kind of crime,' Hanataka shoots him down.

'You both could be wrong and an assailant may simply have assumed the blade to be of value,' Amatsuda interjects. 'The truth is, we don't know the reason for the theft and as such we should be extra vigilant in light of the death of two of our comrades.'

The others all state their agreement with Amatsuda's thoughts and decide on how best to plan for coming events and the funeral.

'Princess,' Jingoro attracts Kagome's attention after the others have left, 'I will travel to meet my father in the Uesugi clan and get his blessing for my proposal. I know that our marriage will give us a tactical advantage and I can help you find new land for your clan once this is finally all over. Hold back Yamatsuru-san's and the Old Man's funeral until I return.'

'Please hurry, Jingoro-san. I fear the same fate would await you if you dally.' Kagome places her hands on Jingoro's cheeks as she bids him a safe journey.

Once Jingoro has left and Kagome has made sure that she is alone with Amatsuda, she utters quietly to him: 'I fear there may be another reason behind Turtle-san's passing, Amatsuda-san.'

'Princess?'

'We have never seen his face, how can we be certain the man who has been murdered is Turtle-san?'

The morning has drawn on and Kagome has retreated to her room to study. She sits in seiza, quietly reading a long scroll laid out on her lap. She finds herself unable to focus; instead her mind drifts to thoughts on her parents, her betrothed and her murdered friends.

A knock comes from the wooden floor in the hall outside her room, rousing her from her daydreams.

'Please, come in,' Kagome calls to the door behind her. A response comes in the sound of the door sliding open and shut again in a swift moment.

'What would you like to discuss?' she asks, still facing away from her guest. No response sounds.

'What is the ma—' Before she has the chance to turn her head towards the guest, she is stopped by a sharp pain piercing her back.

She coughs.

Blood comes forth from the back of her throat, splattering on the scroll in front of her.

She looks down.

Through hazy eyes she sees a sword blade protruding from the centre of her chest.

As her blood drips from the blade, it flows away from a marking that she knows.

It's a crest.

A crest from one of the men who serve her loyally.

Her eyes well up as the realisation takes hold.

The sword is swiftly removed from her body and she chokes on her blood once again.
She falls to the side and her tears flow down her cheeks.
She wills her voice to call out her killer's name.
But she remains silent – as the inky blackness of death steals her soul away to higan.

後ろの正面だあれ
Ushiro no shoumen daare?

I'll Tell You No Lies
Tori Jeffs

What your Mother told you about my disappearance was a lie. You do believe that, don't you? I didn't just up and leave of my own accord. I was forced out, banished, if you like. She informed me I was no longer required in your life and I should pack up my things and just go. The most painful part of it all was coming home early one afternoon and actually witnessing the event that led to my sudden departure. I had thought it would be nice to knock off work early that day and take you to the park to feed the ducks. I instead arrived home to experience my own personal hell, and see your Mother going at it, hammer and tongs. No, not what you're thinking young man!

I heard the shouting first and when I entered the playroom I saw her striking you so hard your little body lifted off the ground and jerked across the room like a discarded toy. You were less than a year old. I flinched at the same instant you did, but my recovery was quicker. Without a moment's hesitation I took the two strides from the door to reach her... and I struck her. You couldn't fight back so I did it for you; I had to stop the madness unravelling any further. I expected her to back down then, purely from the shock of me hitting her, as I had never raised so much as an eyebrow at her before. But her anger had gathered too much momentum I suppose, for she came at me, like a woman possessed. Bizarrely, I could hear a bell ringing in my mind in that instant, signalling 'Round 2!' of the fight. I had to cross my arms in front of my face and cover my sides to deflect her vicious blows. I remember being surprised at her physical strength, but then I've always underestimated her. I saw you hiding behind an armchair and felt grateful her anger was focused on me and not you, but I died a little inside when I realised you would probably remember that scene for the rest of your life.

Afterwards, when she was spent, and I had settled you to sleep, she asked me a most peculiar question, 'Why did you do it

Peter?' I had held my silence up to that point, still processing what I had seen. But then I broke down, or rather, broke out.

My thundering response was, 'Why? WHY? Why WHAT Jacinda? Why did I marry you in the first place? Why did I come home early this afternoon to catch you battering the hell out of our little boy? Or why did I hit you and let you hit me? Which bloody why do you want me to answer, you disgusting excuse for a human being?' Your Mother went quiet then; for once, she didn't have the balls to look me in the eye and answer. I loved her once, deeply, but at that moment I don't think I could have loathed another person more in my life. I had to walk away then Son, lest I hit her again. But you...you deserve the answers to those questions and I implore you to hear me out before you pass final judgement on me, and my absence, all these years.

I was a weak man. I cheated on your Mother and it wasn't the first time. I thought I had been frightfully clever about it all, of course, but back then I was rather naïve. Women have a knack of 'knowing' even if they don't know, y'know? When they 'know' all they need is proof and it didn't take your Mother long to find it. I was unaware of her suspicions and blithely carried on with the lies, not realising she was gathering evidence of my 'sordid fling' at every opportunity. But I think the more she found out, the less she knew what to do about it, so she swallowed the disappointment and buried it deep within her, and tried to carry on as if everything was as it should be. To make matters worse, my affair wasn't short-lived – I quickly fell in love with the other woman and gradually spent more time with her and less time with you.

When she hit you that day, John, I truly believe it was the first time and would be the last. It was me she hated during that moment of insanity. She had poured all her love, energy and devotion into being the best mother she could be to you. When you walked your first steps, she went on about it for weeks and was irritated I didn't match her prolonged enthusiasm. So when you uttered your first word, 'Daddy', she simply broke. The bitterness that had suffocated her for so long flooded out and she didn't know how to stop it. She lashed out at you, shouted at you and hit your little face. I walked in at the worst possible moment and saw the culmination of all that pent-up anger and hurt I had instigated.

None of it was your fault, John. It could've been anything that set her off – a broken cup, a forgotten appointment – she was a ticking time-bomb and that is why I had to leave. I knew she didn't mean to hurt you and I felt certain she would never raise a hand to you again. It was me who had hurt her and for her own self-preservation she had to send me away.

It killed me to walk away the night I left. I tucked you into bed and kissed your sweet little nose before leaving your room. I walked out the door without a word to your Mother and we never spoke again.

Now, she is gone. I never got to say sorry to her. And I never got to say sorry to you. I am so sorry, my darling boy. I am so sorry she took your life along with her own. I should have taken you with me.

We Are What We Are
Sherrall Davey

The tide lazily sips the shoreline
While I bob about on a wave
In a stalwart bath
For all to share.
Spying visitors, spying me
Preening!
What a chore
People, such a bore.
Looking our best
Majestic, of course
Heads held high
Strutting like lifeguards.
It starts, the scraps
As if we are hungry rats
More to me
We're orchids of the sea,
Taking to the wing
Warm air flows bring.
Screaming on high
Owning the sky
Knowing what it means to fly.

Unfinished Painting
By 'Canvas'
Helen Robinson

I came into the world naked and you clothed me,
But I could never choose or guess my finery,
Only follow your movements and decisions
And then surrender
To the shades, textures, brush marks and raw energy.
You loved me so, and painted my first quarter curves:
(My bottom left – your bottom right)
An abstract design in vibrant yellows and purples.

I was unfinished and you left me
My cheeks shone oil-tacky for days.
I missed your screwed eyes, calloused thumb and held breath;
Never really understood your vision.
How could !? Three quarters empty?

I remained loyal, cooperative, proud even.
I knew you would return to haunt me.
You said it had been your two cataracts.
You accused me of having changed beyond redemption,
And banned me to the greenhouse.
But it was *your* new eyes that changed my colours—
I knew I had not faded, turquoised or flaked.

I waited patiently for you to pick up your life again,
Ease away the contrast, the evidence, the frustration
And relax into my qualities,
Recollecting cohesion.

But your anger grew personal, shaky and irrational,
And you daubed me with hurtful smudges
And cut my other three corners with crooked lines.
Helpless, I was watching a kind of exorcism.
'I am so sorry,' we whispered,
'I have been such a burden to you.
We have both tried so hard.'

Then someone hung me in a public lounge
For two years, redecorated, then rehung me.
But later I was neglected, overheated and finally lost.
Builders had thrown me, badly warped, into a skip.
By chance a kind nurse found me there,
Rescued and straightened me with great care but NO...
You had already left me again...
        ...and this time you had died!

But I love my Creator still.

This is a true story of John's last canvas, 4ft x 3ft, 2004, now safe in my garage.

We are a Grandmother
Pamela Kaye

You know that old biddy at the bus stop who hones in on you, maybe because you've got a kind face, look as if you haven't got a life? Anyway, she looms into sight muttering something uplifting about the rotten weather, the rubbish bus service or her throbbing corns. Eventually, she will ask one of the two questions you were dreading when you first spotted the old girl hobbling purposefully towards you.

'How old do you think I am?'

There's no escaping this one.

A reluctant, 'Sorry, but I'm not very good at guessing ages', will be dismissed out of hand as the ancient one, with all the tenacity of a terrier sniffing out a rabbit, demands an answer.

'Go on,' she will insist, 'have a guess.' So you do an instant spot of mental arithmetic. The moth-eaten old hag doesn't look a day under ninety so to keep her sweet you knock off fifteen years.

'I'm seventy-two,' she hisses through pursed lips, her eyes narrowed to malevolent slits. 'Most people think I look years younger.' Your stuttered apology elicits only an explosive herrumph. This is the point at which you realise that all is lost and that you had better prepare yourself for the dreaded question number two. Uh-oh. Here it comes.

'Would you like to see some photos of my grandchildren?'

Half an hour later with still no bus in sight, you are familiar, not just with the names of all thirteen of the old harridan's grandchildren, but with every detail of when each of the blighters was weaned, potty trained or graduated to a young offenders' institution. Just as the thought of cutting your throat with a rusty razor begins to look attractive your bus finally materialises and you leave Grannie at the bus stop peering around for a fresh victim.

And now it has happened, my worst nightmare, worse even than the one where I'm on my mobile informing the carriage in booming tones that 'I'M ON THE TRAIN', I've turned into that old biddy. Yes, I too have become a grandmother and if I thought I could bore for Britain on the subject of my wonderful children I'm world ruddy champion when it comes to my exceptional granddaughter. Now I'm the one accosting complete strangers wherever and whenever I can corner them, pointedly ignoring their look of wild-eyed panic as I approach.

Meticulously cataloguing my granddaughter's astonishing achievements I am blind to the glazed looks as I bombard the hapless ones with a limitless store of anecdotes demonstrating the true genius of this remarkable child. And, of course, I never leave the house without the photos: Lily in the bath, Lily asleep in her cot, Lily on the potty, Lily in her highchair with a bowl of pasta upturned on her head, Lily smiling, Lily crying, Lily in the bath again...

Oh, by the way, how old do you think I am?

The Longings of Habbib
Gillian Kerr

Habbib yawned, a long open-mouthed yawn which consumed his entire body and released some of the boredom within. Behind his dark glasses, however, his eyes never wavered from the object of his attention – Layla. From the cab of the coach, he could just make out the movements of her slight body as she weaved in and out of the tables smiling and talking to the group of tourists who had just alighted from the coach – Habbib's coach as he liked to think of it – to the cool of the palm-fringed restaurant. He watched her as she moved easily among the group, checking food orders, pointing out the washrooms, attending to their questions, rarely losing the animated smile which lit her small, delicately-featured face. Once she looked up and seemed to look directly at him, perhaps puzzled he had not followed them in to take his place at the table reserved for coach-drivers. Did she wonder about him? Habbib mused. Or was it wishful thinking on his part? A rumble of hunger from his long-empty stomach broke into his meditations, and brought him back to reality.

Joining his fellow drivers, Habbib managed only monosyllables as their badinage flowed around him, eating mechanically, trying to enjoy the chicken and couscous before him but tasting only ashes in his mouth. Still he found his gaze following Layla and the dull ache in the pit of his stomach would not leave him. He felt possessed, consumed, and wretchedly unhappy. Like a robot he followed the drivers into the lavatories, before boarding his coach again, smiling on autopilot as the group, mostly older women, made themselves comfortable for the next leg of the tour. As usual, they were laughing and chatting, eyes bright and alert and ready for new sights and experiences. Though he had driven for the company for several years now, he never ceased to marvel at these splendid, confident, alien women, at ease with everyone. At the end of the trip he knew they would be generous with their tips and kind in their words to him, but he guessed, too, that they found him – Habbib – alien also.

He watched Layla as she left the restaurant, exchanging words and smiles with the staff. At twenty-five, she already exuded the same confidence as the women in his coach. He glanced in the small mirror above him, again admiring his reflection. His wife accused him continually of vanity but the sight of his strong profile and abundance of thick dark hair, well-oiled and smelling of cedarwood, always pleased him. Sliding his hand into his waistband, he withdrew the small pocket-brush he always carried with him and, for the tenth time already that day, smoothed down his hair.

Habbib allowed himself a small smile. He knew that women found him handsome – even his wife had once called him her Prince of Men – but knew also that he could not, would not, ever take advantage of their interest. Whether through cowardice or convention or conscience, he was not sure. Certainly other drivers took part in clandestine affairs when away on safari trips like this one, involving two or three days away from home. They seemed untroubled by their infidelities with the sultry waitress at The Flamingo Café, or the shop assistant at the toll-road garage, or the chambermaid with the dyed red hair at the oasis town hotel where most trips stayed overnight.

Soon they were once more on their way. Behind him conversation and laughter hummed. Everything seemed to please the English: the Roman ruins this morning; the anglicised version of his country's food for lunch; the prospect of the desert oasis visit to come. At last came a lull in the activity and peace descended. Layla settled herself in her seat across and slightly behind from Habbib and as usual her perfume wafted over to him, disturbing his concentration yet delighting him. He was glad that the university educated Layla, with her Western ways, at least retained a love for the heady scents of her homeland. Not for her the wishy-washy colognes of the English tourists with their hints of lavender and magnolia. For the hundredth time Habbib breathed in Layla's exotic fragrance.

After three days' leave, Habbib was on duty again. For the first time, he prayed it would not be Layla on board – but of course it was. 'Such a good team,' the tour manager always declared. Another enthusiastic crowd of English tourists chattered their way onto the coach, some smiling with recognition at their handsome coach-driver.

But it was not the same Habbib who smiled back at them. He had just spent three of the most difficult days of his life. Once back home, so much had irritated or depressed him: the shabbiness of the flat he shared with Mariam and their two children and Mariam's incessant complaints about her boring life at home, limited by their lack of money.

'When will I see my beloved parents again?' she moaned. 'When will they see their dear grand-children? We can never afford to travel anywhere.' Habib knew it by heart.

It was no use reminding Mariam that with the children both at school she could now take on a part-time job. Not having to go out to work was essential to her well-being and sense of status, he knew full well. But times had changed. So many of his colleagues now had wives who worked in the town for a few hours a week to afford the simple luxuries which made life easier.

Only the hugs from his children had the power to lighten his mood, something that never changed. On his arrival, seven year-old Shayma wound her arms joyfully around his neck and whispered loving things in his ear while her older brother, Karim, looked up at him with his usual respect.

But, as usual, Habbib's good humour had splintered as Mariam had launched into yet another attack on him and their 'poor existence'. He had stared at her sharp angry features framed by her blue hijab, and thrown with cold indifference a handful of notes and coins, his tips for the tour, onto the dinner-table.

Two restless, sleepless nights full of horrendous images and lustful thoughts had followed, and changed him. Habbib had determined to become like the other drivers, the ones who strayed, the ones who lived their double lives with apparent ease. Now he was sure that Layla needed him to show his feelings. How could he know what she wanted from him unless he behaved like a man, one who, like herself, had left the old conventions behind?

Despite his new-found resolve, Habbib felt himself flushing behind his sunglasses and his hands on the wheel trembling as he put the coach into gear.

It was not till near the end of the day that Habbib contrived the chance to be alone with Layla. On their way home they had made the customary stop at a carpet factory. For once, Habbib had not stayed on the coach but had followed the group into the factory, standing at the back. In the large air-conditioned showroom, the tourists were enjoying complimentary glasses of refreshing mint tea as they oohed and aahed over the jewel-like colours and rich patterns of the carpets and rugs being flung theatrically at their feet.

He was aware of Layla looking behind her at him, and when the group was fully occupied, she beckoned for him to follow her through a door marked 'Private', leading to the company offices.

Once through the door she turned to face him with a look of concern on her face. 'What is the matter with you, Habbib? You've looked and behaved most oddly today. Are you sick? Is there anything I can do?'

This was all the encouragement Habbib needed and, grasping Layla's narrow shoulders, he propelled her backwards into what appeared to be a stock room. Her eyes widened as he kicked the door shut behind him and a moment later he had pinned her arms behind her back and was raining kisses on her face. 'You know this is what you want from me, Layla – you know you desire me,' whispered Habbib, his voice thick with lust. He wondered if he dare place a hand on her breast but before he could act, she had wriggled out of his grasp and, as she wrenched open the door he heard her quiet sobbing. 'How could you, Habbib, you of all people...'

The group knew something had happened. He could hear the whispers behind him in the coach. The atmosphere was palpable. Opposite him Layla sat in her usual seat, dark sunglasses firmly in place, focusing hard on the papers in her lap. Habbib started the engine and the coach rumbled forward. He turned on the windscreen wipers to clean off the dust of the day and as drops of moisture spread across the window he felt hot tears of humiliation begin to stream down his face.

The Pianist
Sue Smith

The last of the mourners have gone. I look around the empty room, memories crowding in on me, pushing and joggling for position in my brain. Some are so painful and I try to push them to the back of my mind. Some are bitter-sweet.

For a moment I dwell on them and allow them freedom to roam around in my head, the pictures flashing through my mind's eye. I hear the voices of my aunt and uncle as they enjoy the family gatherings once held in this very room. Then, the pictures fade, once again the room falls silent and I stand here. I am quite alone. I look across the room and see the piano standing in the corner, the top graced with a lace cloth over it, and my family gaze down at me from the framed photos that are standing on it. Moments of my life, captured in time, a gallery of sepia-coloured memories. The piano draws me closer, I feel the power of the music that has come from it, when my aunt has run her long fingers over it, pulling emotions from me that I barely recognise in myself. It makes me shudder and I feel cold, cold air wafting over me, covering me, raising goose-bumps. My whole body physically aches with the desire to play.

I pull the piano stool out and sit on it gingerly, my eyes drawn to the closed lid. The music rest, hanging, bare of music sheets, while the keys under it are hidden, buried and silent. I feel regret, a longing that now can never be fulfilled. How often had Aunt Maud asked me to play with her? How often had she asked me to share in her passion for the feel and sound of the piano? How many times had I told her, 'Too busy today Aunt, perhaps tomorrow?' I would see the light of disappointment in her eyes, now, there will be no more tomorrows. No more sitting and listening to the rise and fall of the music, as Aunt Maud put herself into her playing, her passion washing over me. No more opportunities to play a duet with her at Christmas, to play Auld Lang Syne as the chimes of a new year ring out.

My throat aches with unshed tears; my fingers tingle with the desire to play once more, to see the unashamed look of pride in my aunt's face as she listens to me. Slowly, I lift the lid and expose the keys to the light. I stretch out my fingers and flex them. I place them on the keys and begin to play. I resolve to improve and let my aunt's legacy be remembered, through my own new passion to play. Perhaps in the music halls of heaven she will hear me.

Then from the back of the room I feel a blast of icy-cold air. My nose detects the fragrance of lilies and it fills the space around me. In the corner of my eye I see a mist begin to form. It's like a cloud, swirling and drifting. I see a form gradually taking shape. The hairs on the back of my neck stand up and I am amazed to see the shape beginning to look solid. Now my aunt is standing beside me. She smiles at me and takes her place on the stool next to me. I look at her and I see the long-remembered twinkle in her eyes, alive and dancing with merriment. She raises her hands and then slowly she lowers them, fingers reaching to the keys. I look up, and there is sheet music now sitting on the music rest. My eyes follow the notes and my hands join with my aunt's. Together we play, the music rising and falling, filling my head. The piece reaches its conclusion, a crescendo of notes falling around me like autumn leaves, the touch soft as they float away, dying in the barrenness of the room. I look to my aunt and she smiles at me, her gaze gentle and forgiving.

The sound of the door opening distracts me and I turn. I see my friend coming in, her face a wreath of smiles that reach her eyes. I stand, then I move towards her and I am enveloped in her warm, loving arms.

I look toward the piano and my aunt, but the mist is clearing. She begins to fade away from my view. She raises her hand to her face, kisses it, then blows her kiss to me, across space and time. She waves, and then she is gone.

The flood-gates open and my tears begin to fall. At first it is gentle, then a sob catches in my throat and I begin to wail. The outpouring of my grief echoes around the room, bouncing off the walls and hitting my mind with the sound. My ears hear the wailing as if from a distance. Fluid runs out of my nose and down my face, my tears now a torrent of pain. I collapse to the floor, my friend guiding me there, still holding on to me, supporting me.

Then I see that she is crying with me. The tears falling down her face too, as she seeks to comfort me. There we remain until my sobbing and wailing slows and quietens.

I see my friend begin to stand and she offers me her arm as she helps me to my feet.

My friend has gone now. I feel at peace with myself. The piano still stands there, but now the ivory and ebony keys smile at me. There is sheet music on the rest and I am playing. The room is empty but I am not alone. This room is filled with memories that will stand the test of time. I know I am heard in the music halls of heaven.

My Grandmother's Kitchen
Anne Beer

Away from the bread crumbed banks of suburbia, my grandmother, at 4 feet 10, Irish and with red hair still evident in her old age, was the most wondrous cook. Her kitchen was indoors or out, depending on where her caravan had rested.

Inside her gaily painted bowtop, I spent many an illicit hour, for I was forbidden by my parents to fraternise with her and her kind, as my parents were ashamed of that way of life and had become so called educated and lived in snob street.

Climbing up the wooden steps that swung outwards, led straight into the living space which doubled as everything, neatly stashed away bed, built in dresser and the little black stove which she cooked on. This was her kitchen, her space, her capsule in time. Herbs in various stages of drying hung from the ceiling to be later used in cooking or medicine and I learned much about their properties. I also learned how to get a fire going in the stove, which stood me in good stead when I lived in a caravan of my own many years later. One of her kitchen specials was jacket potatoes, but not as we know it. When the top of the stove was red hot, two spuds and a kettle of water would be placed on it at 8 a.m. At 10 a.m., the spuds were turned over, the kettle was boiling and I could choose whatever tea took my fancy from the drawer of little wooden boxes. My favourite was mint and lemon, or rosehip with honey. There we would sit, eyes watering with stove smoke until the top half of the caravan door was opened. We chewed fennel seeds, good for indigestion and with a delicious liquorice taste, and I listened in awe as her little nut brown wrinkled face and clear blue eyes told me stories, of hedgehogs baked in clay and snail soup.

At midday, the potatoes were cooked and my grandmother split them open and sprinkled freshly chopped herbs over them. The fragrant steam, mingled with smoke, was magic as we ate them from wooden bowls. These were never washed up, but were wiped clean with hay.

Ribbons and braids hung along the tiny windows with gay threads. She plaited these braids which were then put onto tambourines that my grandfather made and my favourite always hung in her van, as he had painted kingfishers on it and had fashioned the jingly bits from scrap metal beaten over the fire. A lot went on in her so called kitchen. Always clean and shining, but always smelling of smoke, I remember corn dollies, brass and copper, grandfather's dark face in the dimpsy light, white teeth flashing, rough tweed, and snuff in his waistcoat pocket, jet black hair and red neckerchief, he fashioned a wooden toy with his knife in next to no time and used the same knife to eat his rabbit and pick his teeth! Yes, a kaleidoscope of a kitchen, jars of spice, rabbit and rice, patchwork quilts, smooth varnished wood, lanterns, spent candles, worn leather and odd boots.

Pride of place went to the Holy Bible on its lace covered box. If I ever said, 'I want', I was told that I never wanted for anything really because 'The Lord is my Shepherd, I shall not want', and Psalm 23 was shown to me and I was asked to read it out aloud. I don't think they could read very well, but smiled as I read it to them.

Summer days meant the kitchen was outside. The cauldron unhooked from under the van spent its life over the fire with a never ending content of liquid in it that had unrecognisable bits in its black cavernous depths. But the smell, oh how delicious! Nothing ever tasted like it at home, and I remember my grandmother's kitchen with such deep love and nostalgia, warmth and longing for a way of life for ever gone.

Written by Anne Beer, formerly bearing the gypsy surname of Lovelock.

Dragons
(A flash fiction in dialogue)
Rachel Carter

But I thought you liked ballet.
I do but I don't like people watching me.
Let me check your hairpins. Stop frowning. It'll be good for you.
Yes, Mummy.
Competition gives you something to strive for.
Yes, Mummy.
We all need to step out of our comfort zone sometimes.
Our what? Mummy?
Comfort zone. It's like... Well, not just doing things that we find easiest all the time. Erm...taking risks, being brave, pushing ourselves. Does that make sense?
I'm not sure, Mummy. Do you mean doing things that scare me?
Yes. That's it. Clever girl!
Why do I want to be scared?
Well, because when it's over you can say, 'I'm glad I did that.'
Why would I be glad to be scared?
Because it won't be as scary as you thought it would after all. You'll have conquered your fear.
Like slaying a dragon?
Yes!
But I'd rather not.
Why?
I'm not a fighting person. And what if I don't win?
You'll have done your best and you'll be better prepared for next time.
Next time? You want me to be scared again?
No. I want you to face your fears and step out of your comfort zone occasionally.
I think that's silly.
You do?

Yes. People that want to be scared can watch scary films and do a bungee-jump and be in ballet competitions. The rest of us can carry on not being frightened. And stay in our comfortable zone.
It's not that kind of comfortable.
Oh?
No. It's comfort – as in easy, sometimes too easy. Maybe even just doing what's familiar because you're scared of the unknown – of taking chances.
I do like the unknown, though, Mummy. I like learning about new things. But I like familiar things too. I don't have to choose, do I?
What about when you grow up? You'll have to do all sorts of new and scary things.
Will I have to win competitions?
Well, er, only if you want to.
Well I don't want to. So can I go home now?
But darling, life is full of risk and fear and I want you to be strong and be prepared. You'll be okay, I pro –
– *Sorry folks. You won't be performing tonight. The last dancer's vomited all over the stage. Scared witless. Never seen anyone so white.*
She won't be so scared next time, will she, Mummy? Now she's slayed her dragon?
No, darling.
– *I wouldn't be so sure of that, love. That's the third time she's puked in a competition.*
I think she wins, then, doesn't she? She's been the most scared. I hope she can go back to being comfortable now.

I'm Not Doing This Job No More
Russell Bave

<Chorus>
  G   D
I'm not doing this job no more
  C E^{min}
I'm not doing this job no more
  G   D
I'm walking away from this dirty town
  C
I'm not doing this job no more

  G   D
I first went down old Eldon pit, when I was just a boy
A^{min}
My work boots on, my lunch in hand,
C
Working in a grown man's world
G
My job was opening and closing doors,
  D
For twelve long hours a day
A^{min}
Nine hundred feet from my life above
    C
When my mother waits for me

Repeat Chorus

I worked hard in my early teens, pulling tubs of coal
For skilled men digging at the face
In a seam not three feet tall
My back would ache, my fingers bleed,
I'd sweat the whole shift long
Then wait for my turn in the cage

And another day was done

Repeat Chorus

<Bridge>

   B^{min}
At twenty-two, while cutting coal
  E^{min}
The roof of the seam gave way
  A^{min}
After three long days, they got me out
D
All they could hear me say, was…

Repeat Chorus

Few men ever prospered, and many here got ill
If the damp and dust don't take your life
Underground accidents will
The passing years were good to me,
And as I close the door,
An industry once proud and strong
Is not working any more

Repeat Chorus

Song can be heard at:
https://soundcloud.com/russell-bave/im-not-doing-this-job-no-more

Confetti
(50 word saga)
Helen Robinson

Hole-in-heart babe
lucky to grow up
into the physical teenager
drooling over page three in
sexpectation.

Striving for job, home and family
rings and relationships,
ripe with love,
wholehearted, full-blooded, unbridled
secstasy.

Holy wisdom losing heart
age levelling memories,
focus spiralling on grandchildren
sexodus.

Earth Posthumous
Carey Bave

Even if they could simulate this feeling I don't know why anyone would want to. The G force feels like it's peeling my skin from my bones. The feeling of leaving all my organs about a mile behind me is worse than any rollercoaster. Not flying anymore but falling. Falling means dying. I could pray, I guess there's a first time for everything unless this is the last time for anything...

I don't know who you are. I don't know who I was and I can't tell you what I have become. What I can tell you is what I have seen. In the early years I saw humans surviving, struggling and dying. I have seen buildings standing, burning and falling. No matter how desperate it might get life always thrives. The variety of small animals that survived or the plants that grow on, around and below the cityscape.

The city was dormant from sentience for a long time. There appeared to be some kind of flying object. I can see it through many of my eyes. It looks like very little I can pick up, there are images on my database but no exact images. My memory is lacking these days, thinking harder is harder these days, these days, thesedaysthesedays...error...rebooting...I don't know who you are...

Falling stopped, just stopped. Waking up when you don't remember falling asleep is an odd sensation. My muscles ache and I'm shaking all over. The smell of burnt plastic and hot metal overwhelms me while I struggle against the inside of my metal coffin.

Fighting the panic of being trapped inside a space-proof metal cylinder, I reach for the door release. A few seconds after I pull the locking lever the lid flies off my pod. Even though the sunlight hurts my eyes and is blinding to look at, I breathe in my first breath of Earth air and my body tries to make sense of Earth's gravity, long forgotten, muscle-remembered training kicks in. I leap from the pod and bring my gun up at the same time. Kneeling out in front of my survival pod, looking around for more of the shining space-cleaned debris. Seeing only desolate ruins of buildings and empty windows I listen, staying as still as my surroundings. I can hear the wind whistling through the metal carcasses of cars. The creaking of ruined architecture. While I don't seem to have any other injuries my head feels a little sticky with semi-dried blood. Head injury is bad, how long have I been unconscious? My equipment seems in order as well, my gun is still pristine and my equipment belt seems to be fine. My comm set isn't operational, it must mean the uplink isn't set up yet.

A sudden buzz seems to come from behind me, turning with my gun raised I see nothing. Behind the building I'm looking at however a pillar of smoke rises in plumes. Maybe a few buildings stand in the way of me and that smoke.

Setting off after the smoke a new sound pierces the stillness of the day, a screeching sound in the direction I'm heading, signs of life perhaps? Maybe something else.

INTRUDER ALERT! is flashing up on my screens. I had a short nap earlier and quite remember what I was doing...anyway, I'm not sure who you are but there are interesting developments unfolding elsewhere. Small pods have landed throughout the city. Some seem dormant while others seemed to have unfolded and disgorged human occupants. How incredibly INTRUDER ALERT curious. Perhaps I shall walk down by the river...I don't know where INTRUDER ALERT that came from. Infernal alert taking all my concentration. INTRUDER ALERT! My memory isn't what it used to be... perhaps it's time for another nap while automated security does its job – deploying automated security measures – what am I? Error...full system crash...initialise crash dump... rebooting...

The alarm only gets louder and in front of the building it emanates from, the sound is deafening from this close. Getting inside isn't an issue, a hole had been ripped through some kind of security gate behind a massive window frontage. It appears to be some kind of shop with rows of shelves holding some kind of plastic boxes.

I'm making my way through the shop, trying to cover my ears with my hands still on my weapon. It's such a relief when the alarm quickly fades like the electricity runs out all of a sudden. The relief is short lived however as the first sound I hear is gunshots.

The first pop of the shot doesn't quite register before my training has me on the ground crawling through God knows what. I can't see any tracer from where I am. It doesn't appear to be me that's the target. I have to approach this situation carefully, I don't want to be caught in a crossfire.

I carefully pick my way through the store, gun raised. I scan the area with all my senses. I almost jump when I see some movement, in a corner of the room a small black camera is swivelling towards me. It stops, it stares at me. The shooting stops just in time for me to hear the buzz of the camera focusing, the buzz I had heard earlier. Now I'm sure it's looking me right in the eye.

Hostile action neutralised. Strange that these creatures look so much like humans...how did they get here? What are they? What am I? 6x life forms before combat. Calculating losses...3x deceased 1x critical 2x unharmed. Drones 16x destroyed 13x damaged = re-arm and re-engage ETA... 31 minutes. One of them is looking right at me... eye to eye... what am I...?

How is it still working? The planet doesn't appear to have any functioning source of power. My thoughts are disturbed as a voice in my ear says, 'Satellite uplink connected, communication devices online, communication to orbit pending.' If the uplink is on it means someone's alive.

'This is Captain McCraw. Anyone read me and respond?' I say. A few seconds pass.

'Blake, is that you?' I hear it loud in my ear piece, panic giving a high pitch to his voice between short breaths.

'Jackson? What's your report?'

'I think they're dead...I'm hit bad too, Blake. Help me, Captain.'

My own panic starts bubbling up from my stomach. An army rank means about as much as a speck of dust floating through space.

'Hold position, keep talking to me and leave your comm set on, I will triangulate your position.' I start the process of trying to locate Jackson's position on the wrist computer mounted on my wrist.

'Jackson! Jackson?' No answer.

It doesn't take me long to get to the site following the comm set. Old bullet casings litter the floor, bullet holes are burnt into many of the surfaces. Mangled bloody messes intermingled with metal detritus, guns still warm. Weapons lie discarded. Recognizable uniforms are shredded, once-human features are unrecognizable. I am too horrified to even throw up. Looking around I see Jackson, holes in his gut, must be why he isn't still talking to me. Slumped there, med kit open in his hands with the contents spilling out, soaking the pooling blood off the floor.

I wasn't even aware that blood had a smell. With four of my team definitely dead that left me and one other possibly still alive.

I think it's human. Do I? Their communication devices seem to run through a kind of information wave. I myself made a theory about data waves years ago. Perhaps I could just take a peek...transferring data...uploading new files...communications online.

Now I'm panicking. Dropped onto an ancient planet Earth with only six others, a gun and may as well be some bloody sandwiches and fuck! Why? More than half my team's dead, comms to the ship aren't up yet. I don't know how long I've been here and everything's gone to shit. I don't even know how they died.

Deep breaths: in through the nose, out the mouth. Breathe. Breathe. OK, looking around, avoiding the sight of my men, I see them. What look like metal camouflaged footballs – with guns.

They remind me of the army combat drones we used in training. Picking one up, it's much heavier than I have seen before but it's basically the same. I turn it over and study it.

'WHAT ARE YOU?'

The sound boomed from every speaker, everything that could possibly make noise, my headset included. My eardrums nearly couldn't take the volume. Dropping the drone I look around. There on a pole in front of me another camera looks directly at me, buzzing to focus. Through my headset, a whisper.

'What am I?'

Antony's Colossus
Chris Hodgson

'She tried to get me into bed with her. It was when I was on the run and seeking refuge in Alexandria. But I escaped, got away to Rome – I was not so brave as Caesar.'

Octavian throws his head back and laughs: 'Or as foolish as Antony!'

Now I know we are friends and allies, he is beginning to relax and enjoy the wine. I have won him over, our agreement is made.

Won him over, but not with everything.

'About your friend Alexas.' Very deliberately Octavian puts down the wine and rises from his couch. His hand gently rests upon my shoulder. 'Be assured that you have spoken well on his behalf and I have listened. But nothing has changed. He will be taken to Cos for execution.'

I know Octavian has particular reasons, personal reasons, for this decision, and I must not challenge them. But why the island of Cos?

Octavian explains: 'He committed a sacrilege there, cut timber from the Sacred Grove. I thought it as good a place as any for his final moments.'

'The people of Cos will be grateful for your solicitude,' I add.

'They have been steadfast in loyalty, to me and Rome. Besides, justice must be made visible to all.' He looks at me. 'I think I can trust you to do the same. You've always been a strong ruler, ruled without favouritism.'

Once again, I express my gratitude and undying loyalty. And keep silent about Alexas. If Octavian Caesar returns you back to life and laden with kingly regalia, you do not quibble about the fate of an old friend. And if Alexas ever did a foolish thing it was to insult Octavian's sister, and to her face. One day he was bound to pay for it.

We abandon the wine. Octavian, taking my arm, escorts me into the garden. Guards stand at intervals – positioned like statues. Octavian talks intently, explaining his plans. I nod a great deal and make practical suggestions. We both begin to realise that we are men who get things done. And I am suddenly amazed at the enormity of my escape. By now I half expected to be face down on the executioner's block or counting out the days like Alexas. Voyaging to Rhodes, sailing in midwinter to meet my enemy, was a last throw of the dice. But the dice have fallen in my favour. In the war between Antony and Octavian I am now on the winning side.

Next day there is a public ceremony. We stand on the steps of the temple of Apollo. I listen as Octavian delivers a speech praising me as a friend of Rome.

And then: 'By the will of the Senate and People of Rome,' he presents me with the crown of David. Octavian does not place it upon my head but graciously allows me to raise it high, for all to see. Then, with my own hands, I crown myself King of Judea. Octavian's legionaries shout their 'Hurrah!' The watching crowd of townsfolk surge forward with raucous approval. Perhaps they see in me a future benefactor. I have already made a personal vow to remember their temple of Apollo.

My sailing is delayed by weather and then by the Sabbath day. When I explain to Octavian that I am a good and observant Jew, he smiles and takes my hand: 'Herod, you have many gods to serve.'

With preparations complete and the day auspicious, Octavian comes to see me off. A guard of honour lines the quayside. Octavian keeps me talking. We walk the length of the harbour mole and arrive at the Colossus. The huge statue toppled over long ago and it lies where it fell, an empty carcass of shattered bronze. Octavian shows me one of the hands of the Colossus.

'All visitors to Rhodes should try this.' Octavian attempts to encircle a giant bronze thumb with his arms but his hands fail to touch. 'Now you try,' he urges. 'Or is it beneath the dignity of your kingship?'

I must do as he wishes and embrace the great thumb, straining to link my arms. Fingers search for each other and feel tantalisingly close.

'Bravo,' exclaims Octavian. 'Almost, but not quite. They say that Antony succeeded. He measured himself against the Colossus and won.'

I can believe it. Antony was a bear of a man, careless of his dignity and confident of overcoming all by mere swagger. That was the Antony I knew. But his last letter to me, written after his defeat at Actium, was filled with desperate pleading.

I glance at Octavian – wonder at his smooth and boyish face. He gazes back at me.

'What are you thinking?' he asks. 'Tell me, I'll buy them with a good silver shekel.'

'Thinking? I was thinking that Antony should have taken my advice. He should have killed the Queen and kept all else for himself. He wouldn't listen.'

We leave the Colossus and I get ready to sail. Octavian comes aboard to make his farewell. 'Next year. Next year.' We both promise each other.

Two fast Roman biremes are to be my escort; they are already beyond the harbour mouth and manoeuvring with gleaming oars. Octavian is the last man ashore before the gangplank is shipped.

As I depart he watches from the quayside, but does not wave. Next year the final campaign will begin. Octavian will march his legions south through my kingdom of Judea and across the desert into Egypt. I will ensure all necessary supplies are at hand and the desert wells are guarded.

Antony has only Cleopatra now. They are both counting out their days.

Love Song
Rosemary Alves-Veira

There is singing in
The rooftop of my house

My memory house where
Are imprints of you

On my mind of you
And a few other songs

Other songs that sing you
In the way I am

And in my way
I loved you so I do

In the rafters
Love still sings

As I sing here below,
I loved you so.
I do.

Seaglass
Rebecca Alexander

We shed milk-musked clothes,
down to our childhood selves
and slip down terraces of shifting shingle.
Drown our tiredness in fizzing green
and four a.m. cold.

The colour of seaglass, frosted
water gritted with sand tastes
like afterschool evenings
when we caught the high tide
between homework and supper.
Dusk called us to mermaid,
diving into the greening sea.
Handstands on pebble ridges, clutching
a seabed that dissolved with every wave.

Now she shrieks in the afternoon sun,
light fills drops on freckled shoulders.
The waves lift, buoy us like seabirds
rolling on the backswing of the waves.
We dive through surf, sleek as seals,
the sea-sky crazes as wind chops into water
each bubble reflecting a speck of blue.

We breach to gasp, bobbing in the surf
our skin like cold rubber.
We flinch over shells and stones
on softened feet: washed, spun and tumbled.
We tread earthbound to the starfish arms
of hungry babies.
She opens her shirt, to offer a nipple
circled with seaweed
and frosted with salt.

Valentine's Night
Colin Z Smith

The taxi picks me up from home at half past seven, same as every other year. 'The Connaught?' the driver asks. Like every other year, I answer in the affirmative.

On the way he starts to make small talk, which I join in with, ensuring I maintain eye contact in his rear-view mirror. The journey to The Connaught winds through six miles of country lanes – mainly deserted, but with the occasional cottage or two abutting the road. A mile before we reach the village in which the hotel stands, we pass a man-made lake, reachable by driving down a narrow track adjacent to the road. Occasionally, this lake has to be dredged for dumped supermarket trolleys, fishermen's rubbish or a suicide. We reach The Connaught by just before eight, my table's booked for eight o'clock exactly. 'Ten pounds fifty,' the driver says. I hold out coins from a child's play set, and he takes them, smiling back at me as he does so. 'Enjoy your meal.'

As I get out I make a suggestion to him, which, still smiling, he agrees to with a nod.

I walk into the hotel and am shown to my table. It's set for one – same as every other year. Like every other year, I study the menu, then order the steak, rib-eye, my favourite cut. Always well done. That was the only thing Lizzie and I ever differed on. She had to have her steak cooked rare. Even now I can see the blood seeping out as she cut into it. 'Enjoy it, Dracula,' I'd joke with her. She'd laugh. 'Enjoy your charcoal,' she'd joke back.

We came to The Connaught every year for Valentine's night dinner. It was there, in fact, one February 14th, that we met. I was in the process of developing my act – The Great Faustini, memory man and hypnotist. She, new to waitressing, had just been hired, and was working her first evening shift. Taking a fancy to her, I managed to arrange it so she ended up as my volunteer for a memory trick. Using a series of calculations, I worked out her phone number, and next day gave her a call, persuading her out on a date. After a few more, she suggested I give up my dead-end job and develop the act to professional standard. After all, she laughed, I must be pretty good already to have hypnotised her into going out with me.

My steak arrives, and I chew a piece slowly, savouring the prime beef flavour with just a hint of – yes, charcoal.

We were married a year later, also on Valentine's Day. After a quiet wedding, we settled down – me, with Lizzie's blessing, to further my showbusiness aims, she quite happy with her waitressing and home-making. Before long I became a regular on the cabaret circuit – I even made a couple of television appearances – and four years later, we were solvent enough to talk about starting a family. A conversation we were having on Valentine's night, as we stood outside our new house waiting for the taxi to pick us up for The Connaught.

It was running late, we were at the roadside in the pouring rain. A quarter to eight came and, fed up with hanging about, I stomped back inside to phone and find out what the hold-up was. I'd just lifted the receiver when the roar of an engine came from outside, followed immediately by a double scream – one I recognised as Lizzie's terrified voice, the other of car brakes under torture. A dull thud followed like that of a sandbag hitting a concrete floor, and I dropped the receiver and tore out of the house.

Lizzie lay, a mangled wreckage on the pavement. I yelled, threw myself down, snatched her up, held her close to me. Blood poured out of her, smothering my overcoat, the knees of my trousers, the paving slabs around us. Almost without thinking, I swung my head round to follow the noise of a car disappearing down the street, and just had time to notice the taxi's insignia before it turned a corner and vanished. Although the ambulance came quickly, Lizzie was already gone. Dead on impact. As I felt too, kneeling there, cradling her in my arms.

The police couldn't prove anything. I told them what I saw, but there were no other witnesses – they only had my word to go on. No taxi was found at the company with any traces of damage, or of my wife's DNA – how they made it disappear I never found out, nor did I care. All I was concerned about was *who*.

You'd be surprised how easy it is to influence the gullible. A visit to the taxi company, and I was able to persuade the dispatcher to tell me the driver's name. And at the same time, plant a trigger word, so that every time I needed a taxi he'd be sure to send the right one. I'd decided straight away to keep Valentine's night as a memorial. To continue with our anniversary meals, even though I would now be eating them on my own. And to use the driver responsible for Lizzie's death to take me there.

A trigger word to the driver too, planted the first time he picked me up, ensures he, like the dispatcher, is fully under my control when I want him to be. Over the years I've experimented with this control – small things, like making him accept the play money as real. Building up to tonight, the twentieth anniversary of my wife's death.

In theory, a hypnotist can't make anybody do anything that would normally be against their nature. But in practice, once you have enough influence such considerations are easily swept aside. Once, during my show, I had some fool running around an auditorium demanding to know where his leprechaun had gone. A leprechaun! I ask you. And that was the first time I'd ever seen the man. After twenty years, I think I have enough control over my driver to get him to do anything I want.

The suggestion I gave him earlier concerned the route he should take back. A particular detour he might make not far from the hotel.

At half-past ten I phone the taxi company. Twenty minutes later, unlike every other year, a different driver comes to take me home.

On the way, I get this driver to stop at a cottage so I can phone the police concerning a car witnessed driving into the lake this evening. A probable suicide. To make sure there's no trace back to me, by the time I reach home both the driver and the owner of the cottage have forgotten I've ever been there.

Desert Island Discs From Hell
Pamela Kaye

One of the ways in which I prepare for future fame and fortune, besides composing pithy, humble acceptance speeches for the Man Booker and Nobel Prize ceremonies, is to choose my eight favourite pieces of music for the inevitable appearance on Desert Island Discs. It's a tricky business though, how can I begin to decide between Beethoven and Puccini, the Beatles and the Stones, Bob Marley and Cat Stevens, Aretha Franklin and Carole King? My playlist is constantly changing. Perhaps I should go for Louis Armstrong's 'Wonderful World' or Edith Piaf's 'Non, Je ne Regrette Rien', or have they been done to death? Would Kirsty think less of me for opting for such obvious choices? Should I plump for something more obscure, more erudite, more funky, maybe? But, who am I kidding? It's never going to happen. There will be no nice cosy Desert Island Discs with Kirsty subtly teasing out my hidden biographical gems for me. No, I'm far more likely to be invited on to Desert Island Discs from Hell with Jeremy Clarkson presiding. My Desert Island will be cold and bleak, a great, craggy, windswept rock surrounded by shark-infested waters, with enormous loudspeakers blasting out the worst that composers and lyricists have to offer.

This image is inspired, along with my first disc from hell, by my experience of working in a dole office, or job centre to you, one summer. My job was in Dormant Files in a vast basement room filled with rows of dusty grey filing cabinets. Day after day I could hardly contain my enthusiasm as, all alone in this cathedral of bureaucracy, I hunted down the file for each dormant claim and – wait for it, filed it away. Wow, what had I ever done to deserve such an exciting and fulfilling career? Further stimulation, as if any were necessary, was provided by six teeth-grindingly tedious songs, piped through an ancient sound system on a continuous loop. The first that springs to mind despite desperate efforts to banish it to some subterranean dormant memory file is Abi and

Esther Ofarim's 'Cinderella Rockefella'. However, resistance is hopeless. The immortal words, 'You're my Rockefella, I'm your Cinderella, ooh ooh ooh ooh, I love you' live on – and on – and on. So, of course it will be the first song to torture me on my dreaded Island break. With it goes 'Coward of the County', which followed Abi and Esther on the loop. So, sorry Kenny, although I was naturally moved by poor Becky's plight and 'walk away from trouble if I can', I regret to say that familiarity most certainly bred contempt, and 'Coward of the County' has to be my number two.

I find myself in something of a dilemma about my next choice, the catchy 'If I Were a Rich Man' from the musical *Fiddler on the Roof*. While the song itself has a certain merit, aspirationally speaking, it was also one of the selected few in that dole office. On one occasion I was temporarily released from Dormant Files to sign on unemployed people and was in the process of trying to calm down a bloke whose giro hadn't arrived and was consequently without money for food, rent and heating. I have to say that my efforts to appease him were not noticeably successful. Hunger had clearly not improved his temper. Then on it came. Through the wretched sound system the ill-conceived, 'If I Were a Rich Man' resounded. In his desperation, the unlucky claimant appeared to hold me personally responsible for this unfortunate choice of song. His face turned an ominous puce, the veins stood out on his neck and his eyes bulged as he politely enquired if I was taking the piss. Failing to locate the longed-for trap door through which to disappear, I merely blustered as my face also turned an attractive shade of puce. This was the only occasion I can recall on which I longed to get back to the sanctuary of Dormant Files.

Then there is Tammy Wynette, who gave such terrible relationship advice through the medium of Country and Western music. First of all, she urged me, along with millions of other women, to 'Stand by Your Man', a sound enough mantra you might assume until you realised that such admirable devotion to that special person in your life would lead inexorably to D-I-V-O-R-C-E. So much for the effort of standing by your M-A-N. Sorry, Tammy, although I have nothing but admiration for your spelling skills and much as it grieves me to betray a fellow divorcee, 'Stand by Your Man' and 'D-I-V-O-R-C-E, make my tortuous playlist.

And now a special mention must go to Sir Cliff, not for 'The Young Ones' or 'Summer Holiday', both of which I retain a nostalgic fondness for, but for those Christmas songs that just keep coming. I would like to say that choosing one for my hellish selection was difficult, but I would be lying. That accolade goes to 'Mistletoe and Wine', a song guaranteed to make me spit out my mulled wine and pebble dash fellow revellers with upchucked mince pies. Naturally, to those children endlessly 'singing Christian rhymes' (or Carols to the rest of us) my commiserations, but in it goes.

Number seven will have to go to Sinatra's ubiquitous 'My Way', given pride of place at so many funerals, comforting sentiments for the survivors I suppose, but really? How many of those poor souls, impoverished, disillusioned, sick and now dead, really did it their way, and for the few that did, how smug to boast about it at one's funeral. No, I don't hold with the airbrushing that goes on at funerals, we none of us lead perfect lives. For this reason I would opt for a poem to sum up mine, Pam Ayres' 'I wish I'd Looked After my Teeth' would do nicely. So Frank, while I am in awe of your admirable breath control and rumoured links to the Mafia, your way is not my way.

Now for my eighth and final choice, which has to be the dirge to end all dirges, 'Honey' by Bobby Goldsboro. The tragic Honey, in common with many heroes of song, dies an untimely but romantic death, a blessing in my opinion since she appeared to spend her brief life 'crying needlessly in the middle of the day'. But perhaps I am being a little unfair. After all, before the angels came, the tragic Honey bequeathed to the land of the free a tree which 'The first time that she planted it was just a twig'.

Now, being the Desert Island from Hell it's time for me to choose an unreadable book and, instead of a luxury, something that would compound my already abject misery. The book is easy. It's a gem from Barbara Cartland with the (not ironic) title 'Men are Wonderful', full of ego-stroking strategies for harmonious cohabitation. At least that's what I assume it to be about, I could never get past the first page.

For my anti-luxury I will choose a nail bar, manned by a robot since I would not be allowed company. I once tried false nails at the behest of so-called friends who tactfully suggested that I should smarten up my image. It took ages and the long, shiny pink nails looked ridiculous on my work-worn hands. They also felt heavy, as if someone had attached lead weights to my fingers. Nevertheless, not being a quitter, I managed to persevere with the confounded things for all of five minutes, before tearing them off on the way home. This was no easy feat and not a little painful but at last they were off, leaving my poor, bitten nails in an even worse state than they had been in before the ordeal started. Bad as this was, though, it was probably not, on reflection, as bad an experience as the first and only time that I wore false eyelashes. It was on a first date with a boy whom I will call Mr Saliva. During a repulsively slobbery goodnight kiss enlivened by a valiantly defended grope, one half of the eyelash set transferred itself from my eye to his cheek, where it stuck fast. I assume that his mood, already brought low by thwarted lust, was not heightened by his eventual discovery of the wretched thing long after I had escaped his wandering hands.

Now, which of these discs from Hades would have to be rescued from the waves to torture me on my desolate Island? Not such a difficult decision as you might imagine. At first, for its dreary tune combined with the most inane, mawkish lyrics, I almost chose Bobby Goldsboro's 'Honey'. Then I thought again of 'Mistletoe and Wine', but of course! What could be a worse assault on my eardrums and brain cells during my enforced stay on that hell on earth, than the song from which there is no escape, the one that would render my time on the Desert Island from Hell a perpetual Christmas from Hell, than Cliff's direst of dire festive ditties. So there you have it, Jeremy, my idea of musical purgatory in a nutshell.

Rags To Ringlets
Maxine Bracher

I wish I'd always had mousse in my hair
When I was born it was not there

There was curler and grip,
setting lotion and spray
and a vinegar dip.
From the well, there was water,
silky from algae and newts,
brought up,
heated on Rayburn,
poured into jug or cup,
herbalist shampoo,
ash logs on fire,
instead of hair dryer.
That would have to do.
Setting lotion and curlers;
hairnet: then bed,
with a peculiar shaped head.

I wish I had always had mousse in my hair,
when I was born it was not there.

Out came the rollers, next morning,
back combing and brushing,
to make the style stay,
egg white and sugar, no hair spray.

Today, I stand in the shower,
dry hair in a hurry,

reach for the mousse, Guerana Berry.
Four puffs to the palm of the hand, to spread on my locks.
From rags to riches, if I turn back the clock.
thanks to the Body Shop.

I wish I had always had mousse in my hair.
When I was born, it was not there.

Growing Pains
Sue Somerville

'Maureen'll go!' my mother announced. 'Do you good. You shouldn't be moping about with a book. Just take Graham for a wee walk along the Promenade.'

Of course it would be me who had to take baby Graham for a walk. The last day of the holiday, Mum and Aunty Maud were busy cleaning the house. Apparently we kids had made it full of sand. Well, if you rent a house in a sea-side resort with six kids, you might expect that. I hadn't said that of course, though my cousin Celia might have done. And if I'd said it, Mum would have told me off for being cheeky, but Celia would have got away with it.

Daddy and Uncle Jimmy had taken the boys out of the way and now Celia had made best friends with the girl from the family who'd arrived next door.

I knew Mum was cross with me for falling out with Celia, but honestly, she got on my nerves. She was so full of herself. Mind you, I'd noticed that Aunty Maud's singing, as she polished the furniture, was starting to get on Mum's nerves.

Sighing loudly, I put on my horrible brown leather sandals with the diamond cut-outs. Mum had insisted I had them, because they were the design allowed by school. I could have worn my plimsolls, but I'd broken the lace yesterday. 'Through sheer bad temper,' Mum had said. She knew why I was in a bad temper – though she wouldn't say it – but of course she knew I was insanely jealous of Celia's beautiful T-bar pumps.

I stomped out of the door, bouncing Graham and his pushchair down the step.

'Mau-REEN!' my mother roared down the path. 'Must you always be so dramatic!' she hissed, thrusting the pushchair cover and my jacket over the gate. 'And for goodness' sake, cheer up!'

I bundled them under the pushchair and took off, Graham laughing at the speed.

The holiday had been great at the beginning, when the weather was good and we'd spent hours on the beach. But yesterday it had turned cold, with sudden squally showers. The small town, squeezed into a narrow peninsula, didn't offer a huge amount of interest and the week was starting to drag. What with Mum always being on at me, the boys spilling over into everything and Celia's bossiness, I would be glad to go home tomorrow.

I thought about the Promenade. It would be boring on a day like this and most of the shops would lock up early. I had a sudden thought – a walk round the headland would be far more exciting. We'd all had a walk there earlier that week and I'd loved it.

'Let's go across to the other side!' I said to Graham, turning the pushchair round and heading across town.

We walked quickly, and were soon at the bottom of the headland. The west beach, where the Atlantic first reached land, was rocky and only accessible at low tide. There was a picnic green with wooden benches, nearly all of them with a brass plaque dedicated to someone who'd 'loved this spot'. No one was using them today though.

The wind was much stronger on this side. The tide was high, the sea heaving: a bad tempered symphony of waves detonated on the rocks, spray bursting towards the sea-gulls, who screamed back in fury. It perfectly matched my mood. I put on my jacket and secured the cover over the pushchair. Graham wasn't too pleased and beat at it with his chubby hands.

I quietened the voice that told me Mum wouldn't want me to bring Graham here, and certainly not to go around the headland. We joined the path and started the climb. I could feel the thrill as the waves crashed onto the jagged black rocks. The wind was coming sideways at us now, buffeting the pushchair. And it was all taking longer than I'd thought. I felt uneasy. Maybe we ought to go back? I realised the path was following a bulge, out and around the headland. But I was pretty sure I remembered that, at the top, the path turned sharply back, straight down to the picnic green. That would be a lot quicker than going back the way I'd come. I looked ahead. Yes! There was the shelter which I knew marked the summit.

I glanced in as we passed. A man was sitting there, huddled into the corner, burrowed into his coat. I didn't like the look of him. And what was he doing sitting up there, all on his own, on such a day? I hurried past.

We were right on the top of the headland now. The wind was shrieking. It was scary. I longed to be back at the bottom. Thankfully the path did curve sharply inland, but I hadn't bargained for what it would be like, now that the full force of the wind was behind me. Suddenly it was battering me from behind, filling up the hood of the pushchair, trying to lift it from my hands. Oh God, why had I ever come up here! What was I thinking? Mum would kill me if she found out.

Wild pictures filled my mind. The pushchair, torn from my grip, tumbling over the cruel black rocks, and into the churning sea. Aunty Maud's screams when she heard what had become of her Graham. I could feel my mother's rage and shame at what I'd done this time. The funeral, the tiny coffin...

I found myself praying, bargaining with God... 'I'm really sorry – I know we shouldn't have come up here. Please help us. If you get us down safe I promise I'll try to be really good from now on, not sulk, or be disobedient...'

A dark presence loomed from behind...

The man from the shelter was shouting against the wind. He grabbed the pushchair, his knuckles white as he gripped the handle. 'Give it here!'

What choice did I have? I couldn't speak. My heart was in my mouth. He was quite old with a round, lined face and nearly bald. The wind was trying to claim his remaining slick of grey hair which flew up wildly above his head. His mouth was set and grim. 'Hold on tight!' he yelled. I held on tight.

Was he a good man or a bad man? Would he run off with the pushchair when we got to the bottom? Graham looked frozen. He had slumped back into the pushchair and was looking up at us with big teary eyes, a glob of yellow snot starting from one of his nostrils. Even if I got him back safely, he'd probably die of exposure. We began our descent; slowly, deliberately, silently. Finally we reached the green. It was deserted.

'Jesus! That was hairy. Whatever possessed you to go up there on a day like today?'

I realised I was crying. The man put his arm round me and pulled me close. He smelled like Daddy did when he and my uncles had been to O'Donnell's Bar – tobacco and Guinness. My nose ran onto his raincoat. I recognised it as gabardine. I knew it was gabardine, because it was the same material as the raincoat Celia had shown us that she would wear to the High School in September. My mother would have said it was good quality. I felt a bit better. Maybe he was all right, maybe he'd just helped because he was a good, kind man.

He released me and looked into my face. 'Have you got far to go?'

He was going to let us go! Thank you God! My legs were like jelly. He was a good man after all – but he mustn't come with us – I couldn't let him tell them all what had happened – where I'd been!

'No, honestly, it's not far, just Landsdowne Road,' I stammered, taking the pushchair from him. 'I'll be fine. Thank you very much. You were very kind.' I remembered my manners.

I wiped my eyes, blew my nose hard, and headed for home. I couldn't believe how calm it seemed down here in the town.

'You've been a long time. I was getting worried.' Mum was waiting...she looked at me more closely. 'You're looking a bit peaky!' Unexpectedly she grabbed me and squeezed me tight. 'You're frozen! Listen, I'm sorry I snapped at you earlier love. There are a lot of us for this small house. But it's been a good holiday hasn't it? You've enjoyed yourself, haven't you?'

That made me feel really bad. My tears welled up again. 'Yes, it's been great.' I gave her a big reassuring smile. I hadn't forgotten my pact with God. I was going to be good, nice to them all.

But then I caught sight of Celia...I sighed. It wouldn't be easy.

Flash Fictions
Rosemary Alves-Veira

Hello

He dialled her number.
'Hello, is that you?'
'Yes'
'Shall I come over?'
'Yes yes'
'Are you ready for me?'
'Yes yes yes'
In the hall the phone was off the hook.
And the parrot loose.
'Melissa!' he shouted up the stairs.
'Yes' said the parrot.

Wolves

Sophie sometimes thought she had been born into a family of wolves.
Everyone seemed so greedy and tense, always bickering, snarling and back-biting.
Then she met this lovely guy who invited her out.
'What do you do?' she asked.
'Oh, I'm just a trapper,' he said.

Viking Funeral
Rebecca Alexander

The sky was glowing above the harbour slipway. Orange flames rolled in the portholes, twisted in veils of black smoke. People trickled out of houseboats: converted tugs; barges and trawlers; hulks with wooden cabins perched on top; an old naval pinnace with a flapping awning.

The liveaboards gathered along the shore, warmed by the fiery demise of *Bluebell*, a sixty foot narrowboat drifting slowly with the tide. Molly and her mother wrapped an arm around the other's waist, watching the timber superstructure of the boat blaze, varnish peeling and bubbling from wood. The dominant sound, over the lapping of the water on the shingle and sand, was the cracking of the flames. The smell of burning diesel rolled over the crowd with eye-watering, dense smoke. And, under it all, the faint smell that might be the mortal remains of Lazar Ganchev, crushed by the terrible force of the fire that was consuming his boat.

A month earlier, Molly had looked from the road onto the concrete slipway, at the old man; groaning as he bent to pick up the rubbish brought in by every tide. She walked down onto the slipway, hands in her pockets.

'Ah, Molly!' His face, already browned by the spring sunshine, was as wrinkled as a ball of wool. He grinned, his few teeth were stained the same yellow as the lock at the front of his otherwise white hair. 'You are back, then.'

She shrugged, picking up a drinks can and putting it in the bin beside the slip. 'Hi, Mr Ganchev. I'm going back to school next week. I still get tired easily.'

He picked up a nest of fishing line, brittled in the sun and salt. 'Bastards throw this away, it cut the birds' feet. Geese, swans. You know this?'

His accent was stronger than usual, it took Molly a moment to work out what he was saying. He started coughing, his body bent at the waist, until he hacked a blob of something onto the edge of the water.

'I know.' His boat, *Bluebell*, listed slightly on the mud, her bows lifting a little with each wrinkle of harbour tide. 'Your boat's on a slope.'

He looked at it, getting his breath back with a harsh wheeze. 'It's the bastard spring tide, it push it up, up the beach.'

'Is *Bluebell* all right like that?' At its best, she was a neglected hulk, her narrowboat frame incongruous amongst the converted barges and tugs that made up many of the houseboats. The liveaboard community told the story of how Lazar Ganchev had motored it across the Solent in the seventies, with his wife. It didn't look like it would make it across the harbour now.

'Bastard boiler doesn't work on slope. Next tide, I move her.' He shrugged, still smiling. 'You want tea?'

'No thanks.'

He wasn't listening, tottering onto his jetty, bracing himself against the piles of weed-topped tyres his wife used to plant up with flowers. The white paint she had applied every spring was almost peeled away after five winters. Molly followed him down the gangplank.

When she leaned into the hatch to the galley, he was already pouring tea into enamel mugs from a battered teapot. He added an inch of milk, a heaped spoonful of sugar to each and brought the cups up, bracing his elbows in the doorway.

'Thank you.' The caramel coloured liquid looked peculiar, and tasted a little of diesel, but it was sweet. He sat on the bench on the cruiser stern deck.

His eyes almost disappeared into tangles of wrinkles when he smiled. 'So, you are better now?'

She brushed one hand through her thinning hair. 'I'm in remission.' He raised an eyebrow, perhaps unfamiliar with the word. 'I'm better but I still have to have medicine.'

He rubbed his chest. 'Me, I don't get better. My bastard lungs, shot.' He jerked forward, tapped a knuckle on her knee. 'Don't smoke, bastard habit. Will kill you.'

She didn't know what to say, so drained the mug quickly, sugar crunching between her teeth with the last mouthful. 'I have to go. I'm supposed to rest in the afternoon.'

'Time to rest when you are dead. My Mary used to say that.' He slurped his tea with his eyes closed. 'Soon, is my turn. You know how old I am?'

He opened his eyes, grey blue, as if they had faded like the gypsy art painted on his boat. Molly looked at the deep spider's webs of wrinkles on his face, the crinkled looseness under his chin.

'Umm. I don't know, sixty-five? My grandpa's sixty-five.'

'Hah!' Mr Ganchev slapped his free hand onto his bony thigh. 'I came this country from Bulgaria to fight in war! I meet my Mary, and I stay to fight.' He raised a shaking fist and punched the air. 'Ninety-one years old.' He tapped his nose with a gnarled finger. 'But not for long. I tell you secret.' He leaned in, although no-one could hear them. 'When I die, I want funeral like Viking. Boat – whoosh!' His hands trembled into the sky.

Molly sat back. 'You want them to burn *Bluebell*?'

'And me.' He settled down, fought to get his breath back. 'She is old bucket of rust, I know this. She will be scrapped, so scrap us together.'

Molly could almost see the boat burning, its cracked wooden superstructure glowing, the body laid out in dignity in the cabin consumed by fire.

'I bet they wouldn't let you do it though.'

He turned to her, his white hair moving in the breeze. He winked. 'I want to be on boat before funeral. Then maybe friend can light a match and whoosh! Boat on fire.'

The sound of her mother's voice, drifting by the slipway with the wind and the rubbish, broke the spell. Her anxious shrillness was new.

'I have to go. Thanks for the tea.'

When she left, he was saluting her with the chipped mug.

Four weeks later, Molly came home from school to collapse on her bunk in the cabin.

'Get your uniform off, at least, love.' Her mother started undoing buttons so Molly sat up and took over. Honestly, she wasn't a baby, she was thirteen, almost a grown up.

Her mother sat on the wooden chest she had once used as a toy box.

'I've got a bit of bad news.'

Molly froze. Maybe it was the blood test results...

'You know old Mr Ganchev? Well, he went into hospital last night. It looked like pneumonia, but...anyway, he died this afternoon.'

Molly blew out a sigh of relief. 'Well, he was really old.'

'The thing is, I promised to sort out his funeral. He wanted to be laid out in *Bluebell*, then go down to the crematorium the next morning.' She shrugged. 'It's a Bulgarian custom, apparently.'

Three days later, Molly watched Mr Ganchev's body, wrapped in a blanket, stretchered out to *Bluebell* and lifted through the narrow cabin doors. The old boat rocked gently in the fading light as if lulling a baby to sleep. The curtains were all shut, the boat locked up tight.

Molly waited as long as she could until just after midnight, the boat's TV finally quiet. The key to Bluebell was hanging up just inside the galley. She added her camping torch and the kitchen matches to her coat pocket.

The road to the slipway looked different in the pools of amber light, the darkness in between obscuring the cracked pavement as she felt her way along. She shivered, out of cold or excitement, maybe both. Footsteps behind her made her turn, suddenly panicked, heart clapping in her ears.

'Molly! What on earth are you doing out of bed?'

'Mum?' Molly's torch involuntarily played over her mother's hand, as she shaded her face.

'Don't do that, turn it off...' her mum said.

The sound of a car rounding the corner at the end of the esplanade had an unusual effect. Molly noticed people, in the shade of the hawthorn bushes by the slipway, or behind the lobster pots left on the side of the slipway. Molly's mother pulled her behind the shack belonging to the fish shop. A strange silence descended, broken only by the car as it accelerated along the road. She felt her mother's arms tighten, her quickened breath ruffling Molly's thin hair, touching newly exposed patches of scalp. She felt suddenly completely safe, as if death and leukaemia were nothing to her mother, and warm hands holding her as if she were four years old again.

'He's gone.'

Molly stepped back in the silence, the cold. 'Why are all these people here?'

'The same reason you are. You do have the key, don't you?' Molly could just make out the gleam of teeth as her mother grinned. 'And the matches?'

The Black Swan
Iain Shillito

Out to sea, the dark water meets in a limitless straight line with the morning sky. The colours rising from the waters are pinkish with flashes of purple. Rigging is clanging against aluminium masts of tightly moored vessels over the slow slop of water against the hard stone quay. Mist is beginning to come down, drenching the little town in a soft dampness.

January, with the temperature hovering around zero and there's precious few tourists straying this way to be fleeced by rapacious shopkeepers. There are no crowds of people around, many guest houses, hotels, cafes and shops close until the spring, some of the more expensive houses are unoccupied for months. Restaurant tables are empty, public bars are quiet and rain-wet car parks hold ghosts of last year's cars. This is winter.

I like this place for many reasons, one of those reasons is that the town isn't as commercial and therefore trivialised as some would like. It lacks the shiny artificiality of the posh resorts. You don't have to look far for peeling paintwork, rising damp, rusting second-hand cars and provincial fashions. The shops and cafes look recently old fashioned rather than chic retrospective. We are in a backwater, not without its charms and always interesting in places.

Just on the edge of town, a little beyond the quayside, the path follows the edge of the river. Out here with my camera, I'm not a real photographer, well, I am but I don't make a living from my pictures. Today there's no real agenda other than the riverside and me with this piece of digital technology mediating between us. Subject and object, the inner and outer, I try in my own way to cross the two. I wake up some mornings, well I wake up every morning, but I wake up some mornings and I think that I am very lucky to live next to the river estuary and the sea.

I'm not near the estuary now; some way along the path and much further upstream for a little project, a sequence. The gate post, this particular and special gate post. The top of it is wide enough for me to place my camera on, more or less level. Using a knife I have made harsh cuts in to the surface of the wood to match the outline of the camera body. These have proved to be quite resilient against the weather and encroaching green mildew. In the spring, then again in the summer and then the autumn; I have taken one picture with the camera in precisely the same position. The same stretch of the river and woods one season after another. Four Seasons is something I have recently seen on packaging for frozen pizzas, when I've been in a supermarket. I know that Four Seasons is also a piece of classical music by a composer who is clearly famous but I can't remember his name. This is the fourth and final picture of the sequence. I have no idea what I am going to do with these images.

There is an idea, medieval I think, you find it in folk-tales and myths. Someone will have a dream, or a vision, or perhaps be abducted; they awake in a strange place, such as a castle, and waking up in a castle would be quite a novel experience for me, living as I do in a rented flat. It would probably be unusual for most people to wake up and find themselves in the palatial grandeur of a large fortified freehold property. Well, it wasn't that unusual in those days, if their media is anything to go by, this sort of trickery was going on most days. Magic, curses, impending biblical apocalypse; it was normal everyday stuff for them, much like paying the telephone bill is for us. The information is always there but one way or another you have to pay for it. I think I've strayed from my original course; I mean that in every sense.

Well, the idea is that winter, at least in stories, can be seen as a reflection of your own state of mind; barren and sealed off with sheets of rain or drifts of snow. This is temporal; down to the ground stuff. Just one shot; the river bank in morning grey and drenched with frost. Water hardly stirring, undressed trees looking on. Well, here is some of the winter of my mind.

I have a few photographs of my mother; the one I like most is one taken in crappy Kodak colour, but the print I have in a frame is in monochrome, when she was in her late teens, standing with various relatives outside a barn of some sort. She looks lovely with her long ruffled hair and dull colourless dress. In her eyes and her smile there is a look; optimism. In the blank gaze of an indifferent world she has something else, something burning inside, waiting for something or someone. If you had the choice and imagine now that I am giving you the choice; what photographic image would you choose to be the one thing that portrays you? One that shows you to everyone else?

The sunlight is slowly moving down the hillside in a widening margin of pale gold, pushing down the dull grey-green of shade. The leafless trees expose the spaces around them with patches of ivy and bramble and layers of last autumn's dead leaves. The water low in the river and I'm walking along the bank, the grass is covered with frost, the sun has yet to alight on the lower reaches of the valley.

Treading over the stony stretch between land and water there's driftwood piled up in places mangled with seaweed. There's something somewhat larger, I know this thing; the vast skeleton of a ship. Not much left now, the blackened timbers striking up to the air, a sunken keel and large rudder not quite attached to the rest. Five or maybe six exposures, one picture from the rudder to bow with the simple outline of the vessel looking like some pre-historic monument. Light on one side only and; click, capture.

Lives were played out on this moving wooden stage; strange shores visited, alien folk encountered and wild seas struggled with. How did it arrive here? Blown off course by a South Westerly squall and pushed hard against jagged rocks. Sudden burst of cold water coming in through splintered wood; barrels, wooden crates, bales of wool floating ominously within the dark wet confines of the hull, sailors shouting with increasing panic. Or maybe, a human traffic; making its way from Africa via Bristol to a new world, salt water rising among the rattling of chains and cries to temporary, stricken masters. With half sail and an awkward tack the vessel is run up and beached, shipping water with everyone desperate to touch the earth.

But it didn't happen like that, not to this ship anyway. It was built as a schooner in the 1890s and traded out of various West

Country ports for many years. During the Second World War it was used as a mooring point for barrage balloons although I am not entirely sure what barrage balloons are for, I don't suppose they were used much at parties. I read a short book about the ship that I borrowed from the public library; it was taken out of use around 1950, then de-masted and like so many of its kind abandoned on a mud bank at high tide. Although lacking masts, sails and rigging, the vessel was otherwise intact and sat there elegantly unused. Sailors refer to ships as 'she', I don't know why that is. Over the decades water and air slowly rotted the ship away as it or she quietly fell to pieces on the edge of the river.

Haiku
Angie Robbins

First Flight

Heart drums Bones fire hot
Ready now Wings spark Throws high
Grasps the sky with hope.

Night

We lie, silver shot
Eyes reflect a distant world
Moonlight magician

Remembering

Thoughts of her, love-soft
Luxuriant in pleasure
Burn the dark night down

Spring Wind

Cool breath shakes the leaves
Pale green hands applaud the sun
Demanding encore

Black Lord of Eagles
Ben Blake

Chapter One

He saw them coming, two men where both common sense and piety said they should not be.

There was no point in going to meet them. Snow lay deep around the cabin, all the way down to the pine trees on the slopes below, where it thinned and then petered out into patches of ice. He could see that far clearly in the mountain air. Closer, the two men waded chest-deep through the snow. The larger of them had forged ahead, breaking a path with great sweeps of his arms. Behind him, the other man paused to rest, moving so that the blue robe of a *kura* showed for a moment beneath his heavy fleece.

So. One priest, and a big man with him. Where they should not be.

Then the larger man looked up as well, and Kai a flash of surprise.

That was Matlal. He would swear it by the Eyeless God. Matlal, here at the retreat, disturbing Kai's solitude. And a priest with him, which meant Matlal hadn't simply sneaked past the temple in the valley below. That in turn meant that something was very wrong. The *kura* never allowed contemplation to be disturbed.

Kai sat, thinking.

After a time he stood up and went inside the cabin. It was a single small room carved into the face of a cliff, with a narrow door and high window. A bronze pipe ran down from there to the stove, which was lit, as always. Warmth was precious here, alone in the grip of winter. Kai dropped a handful of wood chips on the flames and set a pot of water over it, and he waited.

It was almost an hour before he heard footsteps dragging through snow. Someone swore under his breath: not Matlal, which meant this was a priest prone to vulgarity. There was only one priest at the Retreat like that.

'Come in,' he called, before his visitors had time to speak. The cursing outside stopped.

Then the door was pushed open, and Matlal's eyes found Kai as he ducked under the lintel. Behind him Nata stepped inside, a much smaller man, his blue robe showing through his coat. He glanced at Kai and turned towards the fire, throwing back his hood to reveal ragged white hair.

'Good afternoon,' Kai said to the men who had interrupted his communion. 'There's a jug of elderberry tea on the side. You should drink before we speak.'

'There is no time,' Matlal said gruffly. '*Kamachi*, we must go—'

'Patience,' Nata said. He smiled, though Matlal didn't turn to see it. 'When you're my age, you learn to appreciate warmth a little more. Tea would be very good right now. Tezcata's balls, it's cold.'

Matlal scowled, but after a moment he gave a curt nod. He knew how insistent the *kura* could be, of course. The fact that he was here at all, breaking into Kai's contemplation, was testament to his own determination. Whatever had driven him through the snows must be important in the extreme. Part of Kai was eager to learn what it was.

The greater part remained calm, willing to wait while his friends warmed their hands. One did not spend half a lifetime with the priests without learning to be patient.

Still, something inside him stirred uneasily. *Kamachi*. Servant, in the ancient tongue. A title that meant nothing much. And yet, a title that had shaped Kai's life from the moment he had come into the world, when the midwife had wiped away blood to reveal a birthmark the colour of wine, a serpent that almost encircled his left eye. Few children bore that mark: one a generation, perhaps, and sometimes less. Those who did were very close to sacred. Servants indeed, but sworn to the god alone.

Matlal rarely called him by that name. That he did so now only emphasised what Kai already knew: something was wrong. He reached for his cup to hide any hint of his concern.

The big man took a sip of tea. He watched Nata from the corner of his eye, and waited for the priest to take a sip too. As soon as he did, Matlal spoke.

'Kai, you have to come back with me,' he said.

Nata lifted a hand. 'If you will allow it, I should speak first, I think.' Matlal fell silent, scowling. 'Thank you. Kai, a month ago a message runner came to the Retreat with a missive for you. You were six weeks into your contemplation by then, so naturally we didn't allow him in.'

'Quite proper,' he murmured.

Nata nodded. 'He left, but later a second runner came, and demanded entrance rather insistently. He woke half the priests an hour before dawn, banging on the gates.' A smile crinkled the corners of his mouth. 'We had to tie him to a bed before he promised not to force a way through the Retreat. When he finally left, he told us the Qapac Ashir would be extremely angry with us.'

Kai waited.

'And two days ago Matlal here appeared,' Nata went on. 'With orders from the Qapac Ashir that he was to be allowed through at once, without regard for any objections we *kura* might have.' A frown deepened lines around his eyes. 'I've never heard of such a thing. To treat us so, and in our own Retreat! The Qapac is our king, but he has no authority over the priests.'

'It was necessary,' Matlal said. 'The king will make whatever atonements are needed to appease the gods.'

'Even so,' Nata muttered. 'We shouldn't have let you come here. Still,' he leaned one shoulder against a stone wall, 'here we are. Tell us this news that cannot wait.'

Kai hid his surprise. None of the *kura* knew this news yet: the three messengers had kept the secret well. He turned his gaze to Matlal.

'There are strangers in the Blessed Land,' Matlal said.

Butterfly Dances
Colin Z Smith

Two butterflies were dancing in front of Rick's face as he stepped along the biodome's carefully-marked path, and he made to brush them away in irritation.

'Don't!' a voice admonished him from behind, and he turned in surprise to see another man stumbling towards him. He took in a heavily-lined wan face, sparse grey hair clipped short in a retroactive style, clothes that might have been passé in the twenty-*first* century, let alone now, a cane assisting a stiffened leg. His lip curled. An Ancient. A class almost beyond scorn to one such as himself – young, alive, vital. He made to turn away, but the man reached him, and Rick stared into watery eyes, grey as the hair and complexion around them. 'Don't ever,' the other continued before Rick could summon a biting comment, 'harm the wildlife in this place.'

Rick snorted in derision then gazed around. A multitude of plants flourished in the biodome's carefully manufactured soil – heathers and ferns, the guide brochure read, mingled with giant poppies, enormous sunflowers... The place was a riot of colour, and between the flora the butterflies flitted. The path wended its way onwards between myriad other plants and distant trees.

'What's the problem?' he snarled. 'They're only artificial anyway. Crush a couple of plants or insects, they can make some more.'

The man's rheumy eyes widened. 'These species, young man,' he whispered fiercely, 'have been carefully recreated from long-stored DNA, conserved until this biodome project could be completed. They are here so that men can see wildlife as it once was. Before the cities expanded to such an extent they wiped everything pastoral from the map. These creations are every inch as *real* as their originals would have been, and as such should be treated with the respect that all living entities deserve.'

Rick snorted again. 'Claptrap! They're nothing more than machines!' Turning away from the old man he swatted at the butterflies, still performing their graceful dance. One escaped his swipe but the other took the full force of the blow and dropped to the ground where it lay twitching. With a satisfied sneer Rick lifted his foot and ground the insect under his heel.

He felt the old man grab his shoulder and wheeled round, knocking the hand away. 'Shag off!' he snarled, and gave a tremendous shove to the man's chest sending him, like the butterfly, crashing to the ground. Turning, Rick deliberately left the path and stomped away through the ferns, crushing them uncaringly under his feet.

As he went, he heard the man call in a quavering voice, 'You will regret that, young man, I assure you.' He stamped on, ignoring the warning.

A half hour later he was feeling disoriented and sick. The biodome covered 100,000 acres, and the path had been expertly designed to weave visitors in and out of plants and trees in turn, taking in the vegetation and the animals that scuttled amongst it in all their once-natural glory. The route he'd taken, through the undergrowth, meant he could have been miles off course by now. The forestry in this part was as dense as the city that sprawled a matter of yards outside the dome's glass-and-steel perimeter, the trees and plant-life crowding in on him as much as the houses and shops he was used to. This cramming was different, though. Branches and leaves packed the space above his head, throwing the air around him into impenetrable gloom. Brambles tore at his clothing as he passed, ripped his fashionably-bared arms, setting them afire – he scratched wildly at the stinging sensations they engendered. Fronds reached out towards him, their normally harmless feathery tips taking on the quality of claws, grabbing at his face. The wildlife noises too had taken on a sinister quality – snakes hissed close by, their susurration menacing him with the promise of fangs dripping with poison; parrots and macaws screeched rancorously, beaks sharpened ready to strike; bees droned unceasingly, filling his head, their stings poised to inject his skin with toxin. He was sweating profusely, the tropical atmosphere inside the dome creating a humidity that stifled his breath. Bile rose in his throat and, legs suddenly trembling with exhaustion, he clattered down at the base of a giant redwood. He closed his eyes and breathed deeply, foetid, clammy air, trying to force the vomit back down into his stomach. The darkness was twice as intense behind his eyelids, and he heaved them open again.

Another butterfly danced in front of him, flitting into and out of his face, wings brushing his eyes, his nose, his mouth, his cheeks. Cursing, he tried to reach up to swat it away as he'd done before, but discovered that, somehow, his hands had become entangled in the roots spread around him, and he wrenched at them furiously – but it seemed that the more he struggled, the worse the tangle became. A wild flapping filled the air and he looked up, his heart lurching as he saw more butterflies arriving. A profusion of them, filling the gaps between the foliage until there was nothing left in the world but leaves and butterflies. As he watched, and struggled against his bonds, their dancing turned obscene, a grotesque parody of a ballet. They closed in then, settling all the way over his head, onto his face, burrowing into his ears, cramming themselves into his mouth, squeezing up into his nostrils. He thrashed his head from side to side to clear them but it was no use, he couldn't breathe, the fluttering was everywhere, the vomit was rising again, he was drowning in butterflies...

They found him hours later, still slumped beneath the tree, no sign of a cause of death. As they lifted him and carried him away, one of the search party paused, and pointed.

The others looked where he indicated. It was a lovely sight that met their eyes – a host of butterflies flitting amongst the shrubbery. Dancing, it seemed to them.

Reflection
Sherrall Davey

She stares in the mirror
Staring back, two deep pools,
Revealing the very soul,
Her heart an ocean of secrets
To lie dormant, undisturbed forever.
A pained expression
Causes her brow to wrinkle
Creating an illusion
Of tide lapping the shore
Refilling the pools
Taking her secrets deeper.
Fear of being discovered
Sadness starts the pools overflowing
Revealing strain to endeavour
The secret remains.
A flawless face, pools now tranquil
Regains composure
A smile illuminates the pools
Show of strength, determination
To carry through to the end.

Family Ties
Jessica McKinty

In some cultures it is believed that the camera captures your soul. Eleanor's is trapped like a fly in amber, in the photograph that should commemorate her death. Her disembodied head, cut out and skilfully inserted, is suspended behind the other figures in the photograph who are grouped formally, all dressed in black. She is the ghost at her own feast, her lovely face almost floating above them. They are in mourning for her, forced by dint of the addition to act out the farce of a happy family gathering. In reality, the portrait represents a turning point in the family's sad history, a desperate attempt to create something that had never truly existed. In fact, it marks the start of their implosion. Only Ellen, over a century later, will look closely at it, notice the anomaly, and wonder.

Ellen comes across the photo in an old trunk. 'Here,' her mum had said, 'have a sort through these. You'd be doing me a favour.' The trunk is a jumble of old photos, letters and mementos that her mum had inherited when her mother died.

'Why are these photos in a trunk?' she asks her mum. 'I never saw them at Grandma's.'

'There was some sort of scandal in the family I believe,' her mum replies. 'You know Grandma, she was always quite superstitious and refused to have them in the house, just like her own mum, but no one wanted to get rid of them either. She would never talk about it.'

Ellen leaves the trunk for a while, unable to face dealing with it. She has been in hospital and knows that her mum is trying to get her interested to take her mind off things. It can wait.

Yet over the coming days, she is drawn to its contents. That photograph in particular speaks to her across time. Something in her ancestor's eyes seems so familiar. She knows that pensive expression, she has seen it before. Did her great great grandmother have a premonition of things to come?

Fascinated by the photograph that at first glance seems so bland, yet hints at so much, Ellen explores the contents of the chest. Gradually she pieces together bits of the family history, finding out the bare facts. But it is that particular photograph that she keeps returning to, scrutinising the faces for clues to the real story.

She gazes at Charles, husband and father, cause of Eleanor's death. She looks at his weak chin and averted eyes, at odds with his almost aggressive stance. Charles had shot her. Was it an accident or was it deliberate? Though the verdict was 'accidental death', she suspects that he never recovered from the incident and the rumours that must have been rife. He had remarried with almost indecent haste, his new wife falling pregnant suspiciously soon. Both mother and child died in childbirth and Charles himself never reached old age. Scandals of financial impropriety and drunkenness, resulting in the loss of their home, dogged him to the end.

James, the eldest, stands in front of his father whose hand is on his shoulder. His eyes, so like his mother's, are wistful, yet he has his father's chin. He is of the age to leave home for school for the first time. Ellen imagines him remorselessly bullied and cowed. He is destined for the fields of Flanders, where a shell will cut short his life.

Jane, the only daughter, is sitting, the baby clasped firmly to her thin body. She has a fierce frown and her mother's chin, set firmly. Ellen imagines a cold and lonely childhood, presided over by governesses, the war giving her the opportunity to turn her back on her fractured family. It was during her work as an ambulance driver that she met and married Ellen's great grandfather. She will live to a ripe old age, leaving behind a volume of exquisite poetry and Ellen's grandmother.

Baby Edward sits in Jane's arms, his face a blank canvas. He will remain unformed, his short and sad little life ending under the wheels of the grocer's cart. Ellen pictures his nanny desperately trying to escape the clutches of a drunken Charles, while Edward is lured by the blue sky and green lawns visible through an open door.

Yet there is an omission, the 'family portrait' does not after all attempt to tell the whole story. There had been another child, Harry, between Jane and Edward. He was a sickly boy, born early after a difficult pregnancy, and much beloved and doted on by Eleanor. He died at the hands of his nanny, who apparently tickled him to death, though the doctor gave the verdict of 'a weak heart'. As Ellen muses on this new discovery, her heart goes out to Eleanor. How she must have blamed the nanny and resented the next pregnancy, coming so soon on the heels of this tragedy. Had Harry been born in a different era, the outcome might have been so different. Here maybe were the seeds of what was to come.

She stares at Eleanor's face, trying to interpret her enigmatic expression. When did it date from? Before Harry? She feels a connection with her that motivates not just her desire to map the future she missed, but a need to understand her own life story.

On a warm spring day, the anniversary of Eleanor's death, Ellen drives to the old ancestral home, the place where Eleanor died. The old hall is now a home for the elderly and much of the old grounds have been built on, but she can see trees and a lake in the distance and instinctively knows that this is where she will find the answer.

She steps into the woodland and breathes in the intoxicating perfume of the bluebells. She catches a glimpse of white through the trees. Then her head is filled with a dreadful roaring. Her knees buckle and she sinks down.

Ellen dreams she is Eleanor, lost in a world of pain and misery, plunged into a despair so deep she does not know how to get through each minute of the day and night. She dreams she gives birth, devoid of all feeling, her body responding, groaning and pushing automatically. She dreams of weeks in bed silently weeping, deaf to the cries of the newborn. Then she dreams of the day she dies.

It is a warm day, the early mist drifting away over the treetops leaving an intense blue. A breeze drifts through the open window and caresses her cheek. It draws her out of her bed. She is light-headed from prolonged rest and hunger and almost falls, but gets herself to the window. She sees the lake glinting through the trees and feels something other than numbness for the first time in months. She feels a need to escape. This certainty gives her the spurt of energy she needs and she runs down the stairs and out of the house unseen. She heads for the belt of trees near the lake, the sun warming her skin through the nightdress, the damp grass chilling her bare feet. The heady scent of the bluebells almost makes her swoon and she grasps the nearest tree to steady herself. The sharp crack of a gun startles her. She hears Charles shout and a dog yelp. She knows what she has to do. She runs towards the men's voices, throwing up her arms to send the crows flapping and cawing before her. When the shot takes her she feels no pain, instead she feels herself falling and then she is lifted up, dissolving into the sky, the trees, the flowers, the water, and on into the stars, finally becoming the dust that floats unseen.

Ellen wakes among the crushed bluebells, the tears wet on her cheeks. She weeps for the pain she'd prayed to forget, for the time lost, for Eleanor's unrecognised suffering and her desperate solution, and for her own slow recovery. She is both priest and penitent, the absolver and the absolved.

When she reaches her mother's house she runs in and gives her mum a long hug. 'Thank you Mum,' she says.

'No need to thank me, I love looking after my gorgeous granddaughter.'

They both look at the sleeping child. They both know the depth of Ellen's gratitude, though the words are unsaid.

Ellen picks up the photo and strokes Eleanor's face. Her expression of compassion and longing match that of her ancestor almost exactly, the slight smile an echo of hers across the years.

Going...Going...Gone
Rosemary Alves-Veira

Jack Hamer, keys and briefcase in hand, moved toward the door. Pausing, he looked back at her.

'Are you sure you can't make it tonight, Jude?' he asked, though the reply was forecast in her eyes. 'Denise is hoping to see you – Tom will be there, and all the Energy Department crowd. They ask about you, you know, why you never come to any of the social stuff these days.'

'Ten flights up to be in Paradise, do you mean?' Judith said, nastily. 'All those curved walls and computers are in my past Jack, and I don't care to re-visit, thanks all the same.' Judith ran manicured fingers through her dark hair. She shook her head. 'Life for me is here in the Real World: even the air we breathed at Central was artificial. So no, I won't be there. Count on it! I'll be working on my project for Earth Bond Inc., and loving it. Give my regards or whatever to Denise of course, but I'll stay home and work on my own strategies...and you can tell her that from me.' She turned away.

Jack felt the last thin straw of his relationship break. Just a little 'pop' in his ears.

Jack worked for Solar Regis Enterprises, where he met Judith, before her change of loyalties. A dividing of the ways that echoed all the way down. He wanted marriage, children, and family life. Judith craved career, no compromises. To make matters worse, Jack had been promoted and Judith was verdant with envy.

'Reckon it might be late for strategies... You can't turn back time, tide or pollution Jude...tell you what, you go for your sewage water reclamation. What I need right now is clean air.' Jack tossed his keys and caught them. The new key to the car pool glinted. 'If you change your mind call me, I'll send a car for you. The whole thing takes off for me tonight; I really did want you to be there.' He opened the door, looked back once more...

For a moment Jack wanted to break out of routine, his 'nine to five trance', as Judith would put it. But commitment and the Vow took hold, and the thought barely registered.

Then he was gone.

Judith sighed with relief and poured more coffee. The idea of Jack and Denise was fading. She had misread the signs, that was all; but Jack did seem preoccupied, suddenly keen on keeping fit...

Actually there was an air of excitement about him. She was still fairly sure he was keeping a secret. Well, as long as it wasn't Denise, secrets were OK; she had some of her own.

One of which was her new employers, Earth Bond Inc., were about to make the takeover bid of the year and swallow Solar Regis Enterprises whole... Lock, stock and the proverbial barrel, including that imposing tower block on the city skyline, plainly visible from the large windows of her high rise apartment.

Oh, Jack's job would be safe of course. With good qualifications in science and metallurgy, he had been recruited into Structure and Design. Then, suddenly, fitness and aptitude tests, and Jack had found himself at the hub, one of the crew at Central Control; ready for initiation into the highly secret Core Project. The company vow was one of silence. Jack Hamer now merited a management salary, a secretary, and a whole new outlook on his future.

Judith drank her coffee and buttered another slice of toast. At the window she looked toward the skyline. The streamlined modern tower block that was Solar Regis Enterprises stood out clearly. The topmost windows were showing lights already. At some time during the morning scaffolding had been erected, even at this distance looking substantial, rising halfway up the building. Judith smiled. The city was in for a big surprise when Solar Regis Enterprises would disappear practically overnight. And, as Earth Bond's newest and brightest in planning and implementation, valuable in defection, she stood to take a large slice of the credit. And this was not her only delight.

The telephone rang. Judith almost ran across the room. She picked up the receiver and spoke, breathlessly, 'Is that you, darling?'

'Yes,' said Clifford Byers. 'Are you alone, my love?'

Cliff was another of Judith's little secrets. As the son and heir of one of the directors of Earth Bond he rated well above a key to the car pool in Jude's book.

'I'll be over straight away,' said Clifford. 'We must celebrate – be ready won't you!'

Judith's preparations for her lover were simple. She opened two bottles of red and poured some scented oils into the tub.

Across the city Jack parked underground and took the lift up to his floor, 'The Paradise Suite' – all the floors were named. The place was humming. Coming toward him down the blue carpeted corridor was Mr Bonningham himself. Desmond Bonningham was smiling broadly. He patted Jack's shoulder. 'A word with you, Hamer, in my office, please.' His 'office' was a circular chamber with gleaming desk, magisterial chair, and a mass of screens, lights and dials. The hub of the advanced solar energy storage system that kept the highly specialised building ticking over.

'We've moved things forward, Jack,' said Bonningham. 'I realise you haven't been briefed, but you'll have a crash course: my P.A., Denise Brady, is assigned to fill you in on all you need to know. This will be a busy, and I hope uplifting day. The thing is, we've known for some time Earth Bond is planning a takeover. Our shareholders are protected, and our ecological schemes will continue, but we at Central, with a number of selected personnel, have other plans.

From far below came a muffled roar.

'They're testing,' said Bonningham.

'Testing...?' Jack said... Although by now he had a good idea of what was happening in the basement far below.

'The thrust, my boy!' Bonningham replied. 'The rockets...' Intense activity filled the video screens. Like ants before rain, Jack thought, seeing the white coats hurry about. Some of the faces looked familiar. Shields were descending around a stack of glowing vertical tubes. 'We have the answer, Jack,' said Bonningham. 'The final and lasting solution to all our environmental problems.'

When Denise walked into Jack's office, his pulse rate shifted. She wore a silvery cat suit, the company logo emblazoned across the front: an arrow diagonal across a golden sun. She held out a bundle of shining cloth.

'Here's yours,' she said. 'Put it on, you'll need it. Now, down to work, we haven't much time.' She turned and locked the door.

'Just one moment,' said Jack. 'Are there any messages for me?' Denise shook her head. The corners of her mouth lifted in a smile. Her fair hair made Jack think of summer. He wondered why he had never really noticed her before.

'We have been paired, Jack. The compatibility reports show us as a perfect match in every way. Once we arrive, we set up together, and...well, we'll be at Paradise Bay.'

'Where is that?' Jack said.

Denise took a deep breath. 'On Orion,' she said. 'Let me explain...'

At the apartment Jude and Clifford Byers, now slightly dishevelled, lifted their wine glasses toward the distant Solar Regis tower.

'Here's to Earth Bond Inc., and us,' said Clifford. The glasses clinked and they sipped the chilled wine.

Judith glanced sideways at him in the dim light. Pity about the profile, she thought. Really – that nose. Still, soon enough he too would be in her past. Clifford was just another rung on the ladder... 'Onward and Upward', was her motto.

'Yes,' she replied, gazing out across the city. 'They are living it up tonight, in that well-lit bowl of a room at the top. Jack said catering had ordered in a mountain of food, even fancy dress gear. Poor old Jack – he is so pleased about his promotion...what a shock when he finds out he'll be answerable to me in a month or two! Can you imagine! Before he left this morning, he said: 'The whole thing takes off tonight.' Meaning, I suppose, his new role as Bonningham's "Golden Boy".'

Jude's voice held a trace of wistfulness.

Then she stretched out a hand and gripped Clifford's arm. On the skyline something was moving. The scaffolding fell away. A glow lit up the base of the tower. A growl of sound increased to a roar...

Jude leaned close to the window and stared. Before her eyes, in a shimmer of air, the tower block, home of Solar Regis Enterprises, rose up in a clean and beautiful vertical lift-off. Soaring in columns of fire, blossoms of light, up, up and away into the darkening sky... Her grip on Clifford tightened.

'They're going!' Jude barely breathed. 'Going...' she whispered. 'Gone...' finished Clifford Byers.

As indeed they were.

Limericks
Pat Fricker

The Lady from Pinner

There was a young lady from Pinner
Who couldn't decide on her dinner
Be it pickles and ham?
Or omelette and jam?
Or nothing at all and grow thinner.

The Queen

There once was a Queen at Versailles
Told her subjects they ought to eat pie
Did they heed what she said?
No! they chopped off her head
And the King was left wondering why.

The Girl from the Valley

There once was a girl from the Valley
With unsuitable types she would tarry
Her Mother said 'Flo!
You shouldn't just go
With any old Tom, Dick or Harry.'

Adam from Eden

A young man called Adam from Eden
Went into the orchard for feeding
Eve caught his eye
With a nice apple pie
From a recipe book she'd been reading.

Golden Days on Exmoor
Anne Beer

The Golden Days, the harvest gleam on cornfields,
The golden crust, on clotted cream on the Rayburn.
And muted motes of sun dust shroud the field
Where 'combines' work from dawn to dusk gathering in their yield.
Harvest moon, she rises on the rim
A golden lantern growing, then goes dim
As dawn sucks out her colour in the sun
The golden goddess now, her night's work done.
Golden days of honey in the hive,
Those vintage days of good to be alive
When pear trees dripped with honey dew
We dug root veg to make our autumn stew.
Picking blackberries cycling down the lane
Stuffed our pannier bags with fruit again,
And late on in the day though weary am,
Our caravan is filled with fragrant jam.
Golden days of Exmoor's browns and duns
And golden gorse and heather, pony runs –
Distant views of Burrows golden sands
Capped by golden clouds with silver bands.
Cold golden days, the winter ice on snowfields,
The brassy crust of rutted track below the bank;
And strident rays of sun, low, strike the field
Where cattle's breath, rises in a steam, all huddled, dank.

The glory of the morning, I belong
To this, to hear the Robin's song
And watch the sun rise up to light the day
Like molten gold to melt the cold away
Golden days of woodsmoke on the farm
Those vintage days of doing no-one harm,

When neighbours called and helped us split the logs
Surrounded by their children and the dogs
White gold, old gold, rolled gold.
All melted down to make a liquid way
Along the ribboned road, burnished, bold –
The winter sunset closing up the day.

Displaced
Gillian Kerr

She'd realised it was missing the moment she'd opened her purse. Panic was not something she was given to – iron control was more her style – but when she searched her purse again, there was still nothing taped to the inside flap.

Forcing herself to stay calm she recalled where she'd been that morning. The small supermarket on the High Street, the Library, the Post Office. She'd opened her purse several times of course, to pay out money or to use her cards.

She couldn't remember actually seeing it that morning but then she rarely looked at it. It was always there, part of her everyday life. She didn't have to keep looking at it to know how much she wanted, needed it to be there.

She sat now in the Olde Tea House café. She took a sip of coffee. As usual she was alone. On Saturdays some of her work colleagues met up, she knew, but she had never been part of the crowd. When she'd first started work, they'd asked her to join them, but not now. She knew they thought she disapproved of them. Well, perhaps she was justified. Everything seemed a joke to them. And they were nosey, too. Wanted to know why she was on her own, what had happened to her husband. She still wore her wedding-ring. None of their business she'd told them.

She didn't often think of Graham. Lived somewhere in the North now, with his new wife. Well, not new, twelve years it must be now. Someone else who'd let her down. Told her she didn't laugh enough, took life too seriously. She realised her hands were curled into tight balls and looked down, slowly unclenching them.

Why was it so important to her? She'd never got on with her mother after all. The photo was a small one with a crease in one corner. Her mother had been about three years old. Curls fell about her shoulders and she was smiling. You could just see the top of a frilly party dress.

She knew the photo so well. It was imprinted on her mind. And she knew exactly why it was important to her – why kid herself? It was the image of Julie. Her lovely Julie. The Julie she hadn't seen for – how long now?

Her daughter had tried living at home for a while after Uni, but it hadn't worked out. How could it? The rows, the silences, the awful day when Julie had shouted, 'I'm leaving. No wonder Dad walked out!'

She felt herself begin to shudder with tears and buried her face in the large cup of now lukewarm coffee. Time to go. Slowly she reached down to the floor for her shopping-bag – and froze. Lying on the floor, almost hidden in a shadow, was a small, grubby square of paper. Beside it lay a piece of redundant Sellotape.

Before she even picked the photo up, she knew what she was going to do. She reached for her mobile phone. She took the photo and pressed her lips to it. The trembling within her had transformed into a warm, steady glow of excitement. She prayed Julie had not changed her number.

'Julie, is that you? It's Mum. Yes, Mum! How are you my darling girl? I've missed you so much – when can we meet? Please.'

Fat And Lazy Duck
Colin Z Smith

The ducks and swans are feeding well this morning, they take all the bread that I throw to them. Almost all the ducks, anyway. There's one – that fat, lazy one over to one side, lying on that piece of bank that juts out into the water. He hasn't moved all the time I've been throwing. Doesn't he want any?

Father was in his chair last night when I got home. Just like always. Just like that duck. Fat. Lazy. 'Get my supper, girl.' That was all he said, soon as I got in. 'Get my supper, girl.' Not, 'Hello.' Not, 'Have you had a good day at work?' Not anything but, 'Get my supper, girl.'

I wonder why that duck doesn't move. If I go round there, I can get down to that bit of bank, I reckon. I think I'll do that. Go and see what he's about. See if I can get him to take some bread.

I'd had a really dreadful day at work, as it happens. Customers nagging, pulling their hoity-toity weights; Mrs Barraclough going on at me about Sabrina Fitzgerald's wedding dress not being ready for fitting yet; me having to do the work of two because fat and lazy Eileen, our junior shopgirl, hasn't got the brains to do as she's told, or else think for herself when there isn't somebody telling her what to do every minute. And all I got when I got home: 'Get my supper, girl.'

I'm round the side of the pond, now, where that duck is. I see it now, close up, and can tell there's something wrong. Feathers of one wing mangled, discoloured. I lean over for a closer look.

Like an obedient little girl I went into the kitchen and began to prepare Father's tea. Two eggs – soft boiled, three minutes, the way he likes it. A thick hunk of bread, cut from the crust. Bacon – fried in our thick, heavy pan, three rashers. Sausages and tomatoes. I'd have liked some for myself – I hadn't eaten at all since breakfast. But I didn't dare eat before Father had his in front of him. He'd have gone up the wall.

The duck's not right, I can see that when I kneel on the bank and stretch across to look at it right close up. I part its feathers – there's blood all over it, savage signs of claw-marks.

My head was screaming, standing there at the range, cooking for Father – all the tension at work. A dull, thudding ache, pounding right through it.

The duck is quite dead. A fox, perhaps, or dog, or cat? But wouldn't they have carried it off – eaten it whole?

I gave Father his supper and stood dutifully by in case he wanted something else. The tea was mashing in the pot – I needed to give it seven minutes, to brew to the strength he likes. He grunted when I gave him the supper. No, 'Thank you.' Just grunt.

Perhaps they're beak marks instead. Would another duck have attacked it? Or one of the swans, maybe? I think I've heard about swans attacking ducks before. But would they kill it?

He grunted. That's all.

I search around the edge of the pond, but I can't find any clues to a predator. Maybe it was one of the swans?

Father knocked the top off his egg. 'This is bloody hard!' he snapped.

Can a swan kill?

I stared at him. I think, what with the head, I just didn't understand what he'd said. 'Sorry, Father?' I asked.

I go back to the duck. Should I bury it, I wonder?

'Bloody hard!' he snapped again. He looked across to where I was, and threw the lot at me – tray and all. Before I got a chance to avoid it. Caught me right in the mouth, part of it. 'Do it again! Lazy bitch!'

I can't really bury the duck. I don't have anything to dig a hole.

Slowly, I bent and gathered up Father's supper things from the floor, my mouth numb where I'd been hit, the taste of blood in it. Slowly, my hands shaking, my arms aching where they were so tense, I took it all back out into the kitchen. Slowly, I picked up the heavy frying pan.

Sadly, I leave the duck where it is. I go back to feeding the others, and the swans. One of them may be a killer – but that doesn't mean it doesn't get hungry, does it?

When I left home to come here this morning, I could see Father still in his chair. Fat. Lazy. Like the duck.

In Her Shoes
Nora Bendle

She sank into a chair, her sigh an expulsion of tension and fear. After a cup of tea she smiled at last. She was home again, safe again. Who would have thought such a short outing could have demanded so much courage and determination? Once or twice she had almost given up but she clenched her teeth and forced her shaking legs forward.

She looked out of the window. It was a warm March day. Daffodils, polyanthus and forsythia lit the narrow bed and blue-tits pecked at the bird feeder. Last March she had walked through woods and picked primroses in country lanes. In town she had dawdled before shop windows, fashion conscious, with an addiction for shoes. As a young woman she was an assistant in a shoe shop. She knew about shoes. She looked down at her feet. Her shoes were green, a very drab shade of green, difficult to match. Her husband wanted her to buy a skirt and matching jacket. He liked her to look smart, which was why a friend was enlisted to help and today's outing had been arranged.

One September morning, six months before, she had opened her mouth to speak and the words would not come. She had attempted to get up from her chair and her legs would not move. The nightmare had begun. She spent six months in hospital, months of sadness, bitterness and despair, months of boredom and total dependency. She hated the fact that her voice sounded odd, that she couldn't hear very well and that she sometimes drooled like a baby. But she was brave at first and hopeful.

A clot on her lung was the first setback but she survived. Physiotherapists worked on her arm and leg but she made little progress. Her foot buckled under her and her arm was a dead weight, pulling her off balance. She was provided with a pair of green shoes onto one of which was fitted a calliper. They taught her to grasp her lifeless hand in her good one and, leaning forward, hoist herself up from a sitting position. She found it difficult to concentrate and often forgot how to place her good foot. She had a fall, which wrenched her shoulder and delayed her homecoming. The fall increased her fear of walking. She was exhausted and felt every day of her sixty-five years. Her position at home was worsened by the fact that her husband had suffered a mild stroke ten years before, which had left him with a damaged hand and a stick. Two good hands and two good legs between them, ironically a right and a left, but they did not make a whole.

Today she had been dressed in her best by a carer after much juggling of arms and legs, not as easy as her tracksuit trousers in which she was comfortable. She placed her good foot forward, only a little way, and drew up her left. Forward, drag, and together, a four pronged stick to steady her. Eyes firmly fixed on the ground she eased her way out of the door and across the pavement to the car. Up to the edge of the curb, good foot down, balance and lower the callipered foot. Holding the door for support she shuffled round to sit and her paralysed leg was lifted in. They reached the side entrance of the main store and repeated the exercise in reverse.

She couldn't look up. She must concentrate on her legs. She was terrified. The traffic sounded menacing. A sales girl at the counter recognised her and called a greeting. It was nice to see her, she said. She had never wanted anyone to see her like this. Halfway down the store she panicked. The effort of steering herself between the displays was exhausting. 'Not much further,' her husband said so she struggled on. At last she was in the lift. Turning to get out was a complicated manoeuvre. Assistants came from everywhere. They brought a chair. What a commotion! She craved anonymity. They brought her jackets to make a choice, held it for her to put her arm in. Impossible! Her friend lifted her dead weight hand into the sleeve. It fitted. They brought a mirror. Her husband liked it. Her strength was waning but they found a skirt. She would have to leave the relative safety of the chair and get herself to the changing room. Stand up! Sit down! Her friend dressing her just like a child. The skirt suited her and softened the colour of the shoes. They weren't shoes remotely like the ones in her wardrobe, soft leather, high heels, smart shoes; a lovely green. She had had no say in the choice of these shoes. You can't put a calliper on any shoe. They were flat, sensible and dowdy. But the skirt was smart. The outing was successful after all. No more hiding the calliper, time to straighten up.

The way out of the shop was easier. People stood aside for her as though she were royalty. She glanced up and a pram loomed ahead as large as a tank. She loved babies and prams, had pushed five of her own, but now the pram was her enemy. Of course it moved for her and at last they were out in the street. Nearly over! More curb drill, now familiar!

Home at last! She looked down at her feet as though they weren't her own. When worn with the skirt the shoes weren't so bad. They had served a purpose today, provided a reason to go out for the first time, to stop hiding; to face the world – looking good.

Country Lanes
Sue Smith

I love to walk the lanes in winter mornings
when it's cold and frosty.
When the leaves, dressed in diamonds,
shimmer in the early sun.
The spiders' webs in all their glory:
the mist clinging to the evergreens.
Patterns that shift and change.

I love walking in the springtime
when the clouds, dark and brooding,
create a backdrop for a rainbow.
The hills proud against a grey sky
anticipate refreshing rain.
The trees lift their branches,
leaves in bud, waiting...

I love *summer* lanes – sun shining
in an azure sky. The bright colours
of the flowers stand out against
ever-changing greens and browns
of field and hedgerow.
The buzzard floating lazily
on the breeze; skylark singing her song;
The swallows swoop and dive,
feeding on the wing.

Then, when autumn comes
trees change their dress
to gowns of red and gold,
and dance.
I think
of nights drawing in —
log fires blazing in the hearth.
I gaze into the flames
making pictures
and dream of Spring.

The Swimming Pool
Diana Eilbeck

The glare of the mid-morning sunlight reflecting off the vivid blue water and into Laura's eyes meant that she almost didn't recognise them as they walked together from the pool side towards the changing rooms. But she couldn't fail to identify Brad's distinctive laugh as he playfully flicked the slim brunette's bare arm with the corner of his towel.

Of course she had known when he had broken up with her that he was intending to start training in earnest for the first of a series of half-triathlons and had mentioned that he would be working alongside the younger sister of his old high school friend. Rumours had reached her that he had been seen at a weekend party with this Rebecca and it was quite clear to her now from the way they walked together that they were more than just training partners. She was relieved that she was close enough to a large potted palm tree to lurk behind it and she pretended to be absorbed in the colourful bird fluttering among the fronds, thus avoiding the need to make eye contact and acknowledge Brad's presence.

As the couple went into the shade of the municipal building, Laura emerged from behind the palm tree and forced her trembling legs to carry her round to the far side of the pool where the ropes had been put in place to mark out lanes for those serious swimmers who wanted to do 'laps' and time themselves against the clock. Forcing herself into the water, Laura started mechanically to put herself through her paces. She realised she was shivering although the water wasn't really cold despite the fact that it was only February: Los Angeles was enjoying an unusually mild winter even by California standards.

She drove herself forward through the water, keeping half an eye on the seconds ticking away on the electronic clocks at either end of the pool and trying to focus on the advice her college swimming coach had given her last week. However, her emotions were proving to be a distraction. She was vaguely aware of the aqua aerobics class going on amid some hilarity in one roped-off quarter of the pool and noticed the varied ages and garbs of the participants. Most wore baseball caps in the water to protect their faces from the sun's rays and one woman was half-hidden behind a burkha. Their upper bodies were covered in a variety of long-sleeved garments against the bright glare from the water's surface. Her lap times were slipping as her attention wandered and she realised she had no chance today of achieving her targets. She decided just to complete another twenty lengths while allowing her thoughts now to turn to Brad and Rebecca.

She had thought that she had successfully put her ten-month relationship with Brad behind her; but the turmoil into which her thoughts had been plunged by this unanticipated encounter were telling her emphatically now that this was far from being the case. Resentment flooded through her as she showered and dressed in the changing room which she now shared with the ageing members of the aqua aerobics class. Despite the fifty years she had spent in California, Annette – still sporting the tweed cap she had worn in the pool – had retained her Scottish accent as she now regaled two of her classmates with the tale of her frustration at the travel agent who had tried to tell her that there was no such place as Glasgow and she would have to settle for a flight to London. 'If that's all she has to worry about, she should think herself lucky,' mused Laura as she wallowed in her mixed emotions about Brad.

The rest of Laura's day was overshadowed by the confusion she felt over her feelings for Brad and she found herself being drawn into thinking uncharitably about the undeniably attractive Rebecca. In the cool of the evening Laura set off on a long run, returning breathless and tired to her shared apartment. Wishing her roommates goodnight, she retired early to her bedroom and, mercifully, soon found herself falling into a deep sleep.

Suddenly Laura became aware of the most vivid of dreams. She had the sensation of an adversary sitting or kneeling on her chest applying almost unbearable pressure. Then she felt hands preparing to tighten round her throat. In panic she hit out at her adversary's arms, causing the nails of one of the hands to run across Laura's own cheek. Grabbing the flailing arms with her hands, Laura applied pressure with her fingers and felt herself wrestling the intruder to the floor.

With her blood pounding in her ears, Laura sat up and switched on the light, noting that her bedside clock read 12.02. Nothing in the room had been disturbed and she was entirely alone. Touching her cheek, she felt a slight trickle of blood: logic told her she must have scratched herself in the panic of the bad dream. Somehow, though, she couldn't shake off the notion that her assailant had been Rebecca, an uncomfortable feeling which hadn't entirely faded by the time the cold light of day dawned.

Not wanting to put herself through the discomfort of seeing Brad and Rebecca together again, Laura arrived at the pool an hour later than the previous day, at the time when the aqua aerobics practitioners were again dressing themselves to return home. She smiled as she tuned into some of their good-natured banter while she undressed and climbed into her swimming costume. Suddenly the door from the pool side opened and, to Laura's surprise, a wet Rebecca came into the changing room. The smile in response to Brad's parting pleasantry quickly faded as the door swung shut behind her and a preoccupied look appeared on her face. Unlike the previous day Rebecca was covered by a wet-suit top. Deliberately making her way to the shower in the furthest corner, she peeled off the long-sleeved top.

Laura deliberately looked in the other direction, but couldn't help detecting the sound of concern in the voice of one of the members of the aqua aerobics class, who was clearly an old family friend of Rebecca.

'What on earth has happened to you? Have you been attacked?'

All eyes turned in Rebecca's direction and became fixed on the livid purple marks on both her arms. Her confusion seemed complete.

'No,' she replied hesitantly. 'I think I must have knocked myself during a bad dream last night. My mother sat up late to watch a film and then heard me call out just as she finished watching the midnight news bulletin. She came into my room to check that I was all right and could only assume that I had had a nightmare. It wasn't until this morning that I found these bruises on my arms.'

'How strange,' observed her old family friend.

Laura snatched up her towel and headed out of the door towards the pool, forcing herself not to put her hand to the scratch on her cheek – nor to try to find a logical explanation.

Harry
Colin Z Smith

Harry sat on Blackpool esplanade, looking out over the beach and the sea. The water reflected the lowering sky – grey, bleak, shading to black where the rain drove down over the horizon. He liked it – it matched his mood perfectly. The early-morning November wind whipped in from the west, shafting him through his sleeveless undershirt. He wasn't going to allow himself to feel the cold, though. It was the only control he could maintain over his body now, and he wasn't going to relinquish it easily.

The tang of the salt spray bit his lips as the wind battered him, along with gusts of beach where the sand was driven towards him. He closed his eyes briefly and savoured the sensation. Too many times he'd stood in this same spot and not noticed the taste of it, nor smelled the faint aroma of fish and chips wafting from the café across the way. The café was barred and shuttered now, the holiday trade vanished. The only smell was the sea air, and it was too late for him to ever savour the cod and fried potatoes again.

He hauled himself to the edge and dropped onto the sand, his arms aching with the effort. Slowly he began to drag himself along, heading towards the waves which had receded into the distance as he'd been watching. He'd waited until this moment, the point of low tide, as his final test. It would hurt like hell – but at least his arms still had a degree of motor function, they hadn't yet packed up completely like his legs did many months ago. He wondered why he hadn't done this before, when he knew his body was going into meltdown. Self preservation? The unwillingness to end it all while he could still breathe? That was what was directing him to this course of action now. After the arms, the chest would give up – his lungs straining to draw in the final gasps before nothing remained but the ventilator that the hospital threatened. Lying in a bed, unable to move, an active mind stuck in a useless body. A living death. Better the real thing before that happened.

He was about an eighth of the way. He stopped to rest. The irony was, his body still weighed the same, even though bits of it were packing up. It was just the effort he needed to expend to cart it around that had increased.

He'd refused any notion of a wheelchair for as long as possible. Of course, when his legs had finally given out he'd had no choice – but until then he'd dragged himself along on what remained of their function, forcing them to move although the signals from the brain were being gradually blocked. He began heaving himself forward again, his backside creating a deep rut in the sand behind him. The wheelchair was back on the prom, empty and abandoned. No doubt somebody would find it later – perhaps the roadsweeper in his yellow cart. Or a tram-driver – the trams still ran along the road beside the esplanade, even in winter. Although he was facing the other way, he felt the tower looming over the seafront. Perhaps one solitary visitor left over from summer, perched high on the walkway at the top, would spot the wheelchair and wonder at its solitude. He didn't care. So long as no-one stopped him.

He halted again, a quarter of the way out. Every inch now was sending fire through his muscles – the muscles that had once been able to carry a full military pack in each hand without even noticing the load. He gritted his teeth, determined to reach the half-way point before the tide began to noticeably turn in towards him again. Move, he told the right arm. Reluctantly, it did. Move, he told the left. And so on towards his destination.

About three-quarters of the way the rain finally hit, in a squall that drenched him as soon as it struck. He welcomed the icy needles tearing into his face, his naked arms, soaking through his vest. The wind was so fierce that the rain came almost horizontally at him. He carried on hauling himself forwards, his eyes closed against the onslaught.

At last, squinting through the rain, he could see he was at his journey's end. He relaxed his arms, and slumped back against the sand, utterly spent. He closed his eyes once more and allowed the sound of the waves to wash over him. Soon, their physical presence would follow the sound. Perhaps, he thought, he'd prop himself up again and let them take him piece by piece rather than all at once. He could enjoy the ending longer that way.

And then, another presence snapped him back into alertness. A man was standing beside him, staring out to sea. He couldn't believe it – he propped himself back up onto his throbbing arms. The man had no doubt seen him and had come to drag him back from the advancing tide. He bunched his fists. He would fight to the end of his breath to avoid that humiliation.

But the stranger made no move to do anything, just continued to watch the oncoming water. It was no more than feet away, but he seemed composed, even impervious to the rain that still lashed down. Harry waited.

The man said nothing. Just continued to stare, his gaze placid.

Eventually, Harry's nerves, already taut from the stress of his journey, were shredded. 'You won't talk me out of it,' he spat.

The stranger raised an eyebrow, his first attentive expression. 'Hmm?'

Harry stared at him, mouth open. The man's eyes returned to the water, which now lapped at their feet. Far from a dramatic rescue mission, he seemed to want to share in Harry's fate. Harry too turned his head back to the waves – suddenly, and without knowing why, totally content. The tide continued to advance.

After a while the breakers had passed him, and the water now lapped around his groin, the lower half of his useless legs concealed. Still the stranger stood by him, calf deep, his gaze unaltered on the scene in front, as the rain continued to drive in. Harry tasted the brine once more, remembering again the fish and chips he'd ignored for so long. As the thought and taste lingered, he suddenly realised he was hungry. His last meal had been many hours before. He wondered if the man with him had anything to eat, then dismissed the idea as absurd. What did he care if he starved anyway? He'd be dead very soon now.

He was astonished when, as if reading his thoughts, the man pulled from his pocket a blackish-brown wrapper, the word Mars, printed boldly in yellow-outlined red, clearly visible. Casually tearing the top, he proffered the bar to Harry, who, stunned into automatic response, released one hand from the sea's embrace and took it. As he bit into it, the stranger pulled another from his pocket, unwrapped it and, having held it up momentarily as if in offering to either the water or some unseen entity, began himself to chew. For a minute or so the two dined together, the one all but prone, the other erect, but sharing in what felt to Harry like a communal meal of some significance. Then, having eaten, they continued to wait, as the sea continued to flow. Harry, satiated by the sweet in a way that seemed disproportionate to its size and flavour, smiled for the first time. The stranger continued to peruse the horizon, but Harry knew, somehow, that he was pleased.

The end came eventually. Harry was still smiling, still breathing the salty air, as the water rose above his neck, above his mouth, and then, as he took one last deep breath, above his nose. As he gazed at the sea for the last time, the rain, which had shown signs of never ending, ceased. It was as sudden as a tap turning off. As quickly as it stopped, the ebony cloud in front of him parted, and a shaft of sunlight sprang through, a golden-yellowness that lit up the sky and kissed his skull. A rainbow, incandescent, each colour separate and vivid as he'd never seen them before, arched above the sun – an impossibility, he knew from his old science lessons, but there nonetheless. And then the water closed over his eyes and he saw no more.

Criteria
Rachel Carter

She was the only woman in the bar and he the only man.
She was looking for a well-presented man. He hadn't shaved and had long, dark, greying hair.
No good. She'd always imagined her future husband to have short, blonde hair.
She liked quiet Sundays indoors with softly-scented pampering products, a movie and the clean, ever-cleaning cats. Everything about him said 'muddy walks with dogs' (particularly the presence of his two filthy dogs and the mud-caked walking boots he wore).
The List was not going well. She wanted to walk back out of the pub. He did not fit the criteria of her perfect partner in any shape or form. But he saw her and walked over.
'Hi. I'm Steve,' he said in a Belfast accent, holding out a rough hand to shake hers firmly.
'Oh Jesus,' she thought, in a Home Counties accent, slipping her manicured digits back through his calloused, soil-stained grasp.
But perhaps the 'Suitable for Parents' criteria wasn't really worth keeping on the list now that both her parents had died of old age.
She mentally referred to her list. The list she had written at eighteen, now etched on her memory and referred to every time she met a man:
Where were the blue eyes suitable for her future babies? His were brown.
Where was the evidence of security and financial stability for the family they might have? He had holes in his t-shirt.
Perhaps, as her friends had pointed out, she was too old for children now. Perhaps, as her sister had pointed out, a good companion was more important than money.
She had to do this. She'd promised. She would make polite conversation, smile, have a couple of drinks, swap phone numbers,

thank her friends for setting up a blind date and then never call him. In a couple of weeks she could say it just didn't work out. There was no way she was committing herself to this guy while Mr. Right was out there waiting for her.

Three hours later, he led her into his house and showed her the hall, the bathroom, the kitchen, the sitting room and the lizards. They wouldn't be languishing so lazily under their heat lamps if her cats were in the room, she noted aloud with a snigger.

He laughed too and cleared some papers from the sofa so that she could sit down.

Real ale seemed good for the inhibitions and the OCD she noted with a belch, plonking herself onto a stinking dog blanket and grinning.

He grinned back fondly and sat himself opposite her. 'You've a good sense of humour. I've not laughed so much in a while.'

'I don't usually make men laugh.' She tilted her head, thoughtfully. 'It must be the beer.'

'No. It's not you. It's the men you've been dating. You should always make sure someone's got the same sense of humour as you. It's number one on the list.'

'You have a list?' She leant forward in interest and nearly fell off the sofa. 'This could be the start of something really ugly,' she laughed, righting herself and pointing to a rotting half-eaten apple on a corner table behind his elbow.

'I wondered what the smell was,' he said, jumping to his feet, grabbing the apple and running to the kitchen bin with it.

She watched as he washed and dried his hands carefully and then returned looking about him as if in shame.

He was making an effort for her. She realised she liked that in a man.

Why wasn't that on The List?

Epistle from Headmaster Tomlison
Helen Robinson

(I took my father back for a 'reunion' with his former school 11 years after he died)

I stare in amazement at a car park
    where my gooseberries and cider-apples grew,
    a music room where my bees used to hum,
    a playground where my prize beans were chased by the wind,
    a mural where my tomatoes ripened in the sun,
    the head's study in *our* dining room,
    the office in *our* kitchen
    computers everywhere!

Of course I am sad to see no farm school buildings,
    no cowslip meadows,
    no walnut trees or monkey puzzle,
    no cherry blossom or corn-on-the-cob,
    no grass tennis-court
    no billiard room,
    no girls' hostel,
    no Sixth Form Maths...

But they were dark days in the war,
    when land was soil,
    and crops fed boarders,
    and coal from the black stone cellars fed classroom stoves,
    and teamwork was bleak survival

Now schools from the Mendips come in threes
    my calculus lessons were not vain riddles,
    my chess moves not stalemate,
    my twilight star over the long-jump pit not eclipsed by chalk,

but instead enshrined in blue stained glass...

Now children grow in light
   in special units, colour and technology,
   in a different world of travel, wealth and global
   community;
   of green minds and creativity,
   of confidence and laughter
   (candles and balloons).

But what catches me most, inside, as I take a last look out,
   is the inner quadrangle, with cabbages, greenhouse and
   tractor tyres,
   framed by the old solid walls,
   still proudly standing,
   the heart of Middle School,
   and above, the old bell-tower, calling across the century.

I hang up my torn black gown
   on this Speechless Day.

And what lifts my heart most, outside, as I walk away,
   is the surprise view of Crocks Peak beyond the sweep of
   poplars,
   tennis balls lobbed onto mossy roof-tops,
   fir-cones falling upon fertile ground,
   vibrant splashes of red poppies,
   excited maroon and gold faces everywhere,
   like a meadow of heartsease pansies...

And a resident spirit taking care of everyone...

Whose fault?
Nora Bendle

Jonathon pulled one of the heavy gates forward until he could bolt it to the hole in the ground and slowly brought the second gate to meet it, fastening them with a sliding bar. Until he pushed the bar into its slot he hadn't realised that his hands were shaking, although he was well aware that his heart was drumming in his chest.

He turned towards the house, the house that he and Felicity had fallen in love with, a dream house in the country, somewhere to bring up their two girls, away from the dangers and temptations of the city, somewhere to grow old in, somewhere safe. What he faced was devastating.

They had moved to The Birches in September in time for the girls to attend a good private school at the beginning of the school year. The property included a well-established garden with large shrubs, a group of silver birches, cherry trees and acers that were alight with autumn fire. The house had been sold separately from the land but outbuildings surrounded the large yard at the back of the house included stabling for horses, which delighted the girls.

Before Christmas two bathrooms had been refurbished, a new Aga had been installed, the dining room enlarged and the conservatory and patio had been extended. The Winterton-Smythes enjoyed entertaining.

At Christmas a yule log burning in the open fireplace, mulled wine and roasted chestnuts, holly from the garden and mistletoe from the orchard enhanced a traditional festival for many family members who were more than willing to share in the couple's good fortune.

In Spring Felicity made changes in the garden, masterminding a rose and honeysuckle pergola and a wild flower area. By July the garden was a kaleidoscope of colour and scent. Urns on the patio overflowed with agapanthus, hydrangeas and lilies. It was time to show off, time for a grand house warming. Friends and colleagues were invited from their previous London life and the weather forecast promised a fine hot day. Trains from the city were met, 4x4's were parked in the stable yard, cut glass vases of roses were placed on the dressing tables of those who were staying overnight. It was the highlight of the year.

Jonathon lit the charcoal at eleven. He was proud of the fact that he had built the barbeque himself, proud of every race of bricks running straight and true.

Steak, chicken, pork and trout sizzled on the grill. On a long table set with square china plates and family silver a wide choice of breads and rolls, numerous salads, much home grown, dressings, salsas and dips tempted the guests. Champagne corks shot into the air as glasses were filled.

Coming through the patio doors Felicity was filled with immense pride as she watched her family and friends help themselves to the food she and Jonathon had carefully planned and prepared. Her eyes scanned the smooth sward of the lawns, the edged paths, the profusion of colour, light and shade. Jonathon's eyes met hers for a moment. It was a moment of triumph.

The buzz of conversation challenged the buzz of bees in the borders, butterflies massed on buddleias. It was a perfect summer day in a spectacular location. There was a lot of laughter. Everyone was ebullient. So many of the guests knew each other that conversation flowed continuously and, as more wine was consumed, voices rose. So, perhaps it was not surprising that there was little warning of their approach.

Vivienne, who was always overly dramatic, screamed. Others followed suit, some ran, others were rooted to the spot. A single black and white cow was sauntering up the drive. Surprised at the screaming it threw up its head, its eyes no longer lazy. People running excited the cow. It moved faster. Another cow, inquisitive, appeared behind the first and then one more until there were ten in the garden, although no-one would have sworn to the number. Back in London they would talk of a stampede. They lumbered onto the lawn, abandoned cushions and blankets were sniffed and trampled. One animal moved towards the patio. Felicity's eighty-six year-old grandmother, who had never feared the Germans, rose stiffly from her chair, waved her hat at the cow and shouted, 'Shoo! Shoo!' Startled, it raised its head, lifted the drinks table and sent tiny shards of glass into the purple and pink thymes artfully planted between the paving stones. Grandmama's shout activated the men. Jonathon prodded an animal in the rump with his barbeque fork. Felicity's brother threw a bowl of mixed salad, which the animal paused briefly to devour before it approached the main table. Plates, bowls and cutlery crashed to the floor. A bull in a china shop could not have caused more mayhem.

The men stood gallantly before the house, wildly flailing their arms and roaring. 'Bah! Yah! Ha! Ho!' and other inane sounds. The cows turned and dispersed amongst shrubs and borders, curious, investigating. By the time they had converged on the wild flower meadow Jonathon, who had been running around like a headless chicken, and his father-in-law, Headmaster, retired, saw an opportunity to round the cows up as they were now all in one place of their own volition.

A reluctant bank manager, a broker, an MP, a head chef and a volunteer mother of five and a retired Matron, were delegated to block various escape routes. Jonathon and the head chef were cautiously moving towards the herd when a florid Farmer Brady, fresh from a mountainous Sunday roast and apple pie, shambled up the drive, tapping his leg with a hazel stick, his two sheep dogs at his heels.

'Shep, Meg, get around 'em.' Swift as a bullet and just as direct, the dogs shot past the guardians of the escape routes, urged the cows into an orderly group and directed them towards the drive. Jonathon and his conscripts converged into a line behind them. Hooves clattered on the concrete. Farmer Brady, still tapping his leg, limped slowly behind his animals. Hands on hips Jonathon shouted, 'I shall see my solicitor in the morning.'

Farmer Brady turned. 'The likes of you come into the country with yer fancy ways and yer fancy friends,' he muttered, 'if you mean to stay, you'll need to learn country ways. Gates is there to keep animals out as well as in and they'm meant to be shut. If you had kept yours shut all this would never have happened and I would have been at home with my feet up. You'll have to deal with my insurers.'

Jonathon stood in the road for a moment reading stubbornness and anger into the farmer's gait and set of shoulders. No apology! Not a word! He could not believe it. He closed the gates, looked up at the house, surveyed the battlefield, the broken branches, hoof prints on the lawn, the barbeque debris. Cowpats marked the line of the cows' retreat. Felicity and the girls ran towards him, sobbing.

The only other sound was the hum of bees.

Music Lesson
Helen Robinson

He always cycled to his piano lesson, whistling.
I watched young Russell's breathless face
Spilling enthusiasm
From shoulder to fingertip
Into the pregnant air,
Radar-searching for sound-waves.

Then I saw his blank   disappointment
When the finger wasn't there
To free the note
Imprisoned
Inside the black lines and spaces,
Curved on the floating page
So far above those muscles crouched ready.

    Like the look on a foot
When it steps bravely
Into the space
Of a missing   stair
That isn't there.

    Like the taste of a Bovril drink
When your mouth and eyes
Are open wide,
Expectant.
Certain that the black is   coffee.

    Like the ears of my adult fingers,

Memory fading,
Trying to coax a familiar prelude
Off a musty manuscript,
Air-fingering Bach in B minor,
Playing long ago on a concert grand.

Russell tried to teach me to whistle.
He said anyone from seven to seventy could learn it.
I proved him wrong.
So he gave up the piano
And took up the flute instead.
I remember his originality
And the winking arrogance of his embouchure...

...till one Spring morning
We stopped
            right in the middle of my garden,

Both of us transfixed and humbled
By the exuberant cadenza of a blackbird's song.

Things Ancient and Modern
Susanna Eccleston

The old man sat behind a large desk. His hands, wrinkled and weathered, rested either side of a leather writing pad with green blotting paper that was covered in inky words and blotches: Remnants of many of his sermons, no doubt, I thought as I looked back at him.

He gazed steadily at me over the rim of his tortoise-shell glasses, dark eyes twinkling, his nose scrunched up; in an effort, it seemed, to keep the said glasses perched on the end of his nose.

There was an ink stand and pot that seemed antediluvian in appearance, but in keeping with the rest of the room, and of course, of the old man too. He did look as though he could have met Noah, or at least have made his acquaintance! There were several very large, dusty tomes on one corner of the desk, and then, in great contrast, a small mobile phone sat on the other corner alongside an iPad and memory stick.

The room itself was dark and dusty. Large old velvet drapes hung at the window, obscuring the view of the garden beyond, and the walls were covered in bookshelves laden with books. There were spaces where the large tomes on his desk had been taken from the shelf; leaving gaping holes that looked a bit like missing teeth in an old skull. The whole room had a fragrance of decay, and I shuddered to think that this could soon be my place of work. I began to feel the back of my neck tighten and a familiar pain at the back of my eyes, the forerunner to a headache, I had no doubt.

The old man shifted his position, and sat back in his leather swinging chair, you know the sort I mean, heavy and dull with great big studs all around it, blackened by age and the many hands that had rubbed against it. It was probably an antique, and not worth very much; unless you were a collector, of course.

At last, he spoke. 'Well, my dear, you are as refreshing as a drink of water on a hot day, and you will certainly bring changes here, that will be contested, even if the congregation *are* dying of thirst,' he said dryly; then he smiled, and at once it seemed as though the sun had come out from behind the clouds.

'There are many that will not approve of your appointment; and in fact, may leave us,' he said solemnly. 'But if you are prepared to work with me, I will welcome you with open arms.

'As for the members, you will have to earn their respect and loyalty, which is not going to be easy,' he continued. 'I have been in this post on my own now for many years, and it is with great sorrow that I will step down, but you seem like just the right person to take on this task; and I will help you as much as I am able, until I move to my new home, where I will always be there for consultation if you ever need it.'

'I am certain I will at some time,' I replied. 'You will be a hard act to follow, you know.'

'You will bring your own brand of amendments with you, and a change is as good as a rest, so they tell me,' he said. 'Not that all of my old ladies will agree with me, I am sure; but then, why alter the habit of a lifetime?

'You cannot please all of the people all of the time, etc, and if you try, you will only wear yourself out and be no good to anyone. You must just be yourself, and be gentle and thoughtful as you bring about the changes that have to be made in order for us to continue our work here.'

He smiled again, and his eyes crinkled in the corners as it reached the whole of his face.

With that, he rose and reached out for my hand; taking hold of it with a firm grasp, he shook it vigorously. 'Welcome on board, my dear.

'Come,' he said, picking up his mobile phone and putting it in his cassock pocket, and placing his iPad into a briefcase: 'I will introduce you to your new flock, Vicar.'

I retrieved my handbag from the back of the chair I had been sitting on, and slung it over my shoulder. The old man opened the study door, and bright sunlight streamed through it. He led me outside, and we walked towards the new and very modern looking hall that stood next to the old Norman church.

St Mary's hall was built with yellow brick, and there were double-glazed windows covering most of one wall, with modern blinds hanging down them. Double fronted plate glass doors formed the entrance leading to a hallway, with several doors off to the side. Each door marked to say what they were. Toilets and babies' changing room, secretary's office, prayer room, kitchen, etc. 'Quite a contrast,' I thought as I followed him through the doors and into the bright sunny room, filled with cheerful men and women of varying ages.

There was a great difference between new and old here, I thought, and not just in the old vicar's study.

There were children playing, and there was much laughter and jollity. Trestle tables laden with food were placed at intervals around the room, ready for the tea after the formal introduction I was to face. That had been prepared by the army of older ladies, who loved to mother the younger members.

I thought about the books on the study desk, about the ones on my own shelves; new and old ones, and *Hymns Ancient and Modern* went through my mind. Well, perhaps by this time next year we might have a collection of *Soul Survivor* books to use, and the antediluvian books can be consigned to history. Times are changing, and we must change with it if we are to survive.

The old vicar cleared his throat, and began to speak. 'Hello to you all,' he said, and a silence filled the room.

'Thank you all for coming today, and for the generous way you have welcomed your new vicar; and without further ado, I give you Samantha Driscole.'

Smiling to myself, I adjusted my dog collar slightly, then turned to meet my new congregation.

The Foot
Rachel Carter

High fencing, topped with barbed wire, surrounds the house. I sit in the car thinking about what I'm going to ask Tom. But this is such a peculiar story I think I'll have to assess the situation as I go along.

The facts:

The missing man's name was Darren and he was a diver. He started behaving oddly after losing a foot in a diving accident five years ago. Recently his family reported him missing and that was when the rumours started... Tom was the only one he had allowed to see him in the last five years. The family will talk to no one. The police will talk to no one. The marine biologists have gone very quiet...

The stuff we can't be sure of:

There's a rumour that the policeman who went to search Darren's house after his disappearance was so disturbed by what he found that he took to drinking and was last seen huddled in the entrance to Plymouth Marine Aquarium, dressed in old fishermen's clothes, telling tales of a horrific half man/half sea creature with only one foot that expelled waste from his head and killed himself with his own poisonous tentacles.

It's disturbing and I don't want to do this but I'm the only one Tom will talk to so I guess I'm flattered really. Besides, if I get nowhere no one need know and if it's a good story then I can afford Bella's university fees. As a freelancer I have nothing to lose. Except perhaps my sanity...

He's waiting for me inside the fence, restraining a large, angry dog on a chain.

'Sally.'

'Tom.'

He's changed. I hardly recognise the man with guarded expression and stiff posture as the effeminate boy who swapped Pokémon cards with my eldest son fifteen years ago.

He takes me to a sparse, windowless utility room at the back of the house. As he shuts the door the insistent dog barking and the hum of traffic cease. There is a soft electrical buzz but otherwise the room is quiet and intense. Tom points to a plastic chair and I sit down and reach for my laptop. As I turn it on he spots my Internet dongle and swiftly confiscates it while he begins to talk...

'Darren was my diving instructor. I worshipped him. We spent time together on dives and trips around the world – just the two of us. He had this special interest in anemones, you see, and didn't care for the more extensive dives organised by other people. I fell in love with him. I assumed that he was gay too because he didn't seem to like women. But as the months went by I began to realise he didn't feel that way about me. I stuck up for him when people said he was going mad although deep down I wondered if I was wasting my time. He collected anemone eggs and sperm samples to take home and became fixated on asexual reproduction. Bits of anemones can break off and form into new anemones, you know? He said he wanted me to help him with some research and although it sounded far-fetched I would have done anything for him. There's something a bit obsessive about loving someone you know can never be yours... I hung on his every word, agreed with everything he said, became as passionate as I could about everything he was passionate about.'

I nod. I know all about misguided loyalty. 'I've seen photos. He was quite something,' I say.

'*Was*? He's not dead.'

I fumble, not wanting to stop him talking. Then I remember the rumours. 'He changed though? Put on weight? Grew pale?'

'In the early days, when we first started going off on our own, the other divers said he must have suffered decompression sickness because his face swelled up and he forgot people's names. But he told me he didn't dive deep enough.'

'Weren't you with him?'

'I was on the boat.'

'So he might have. Didn't he suffer from weak joints too?'

'It wasn't that though. He knew what he was doing.'

Now, I've researched the bends and it sounds to me that – as it went untreated – that was exactly what brought about his madness and demise but I feel I am on the brink of something so I wait.

Tom seems to read my mind. 'Just because someone displays the symptoms of something doesn't mean that is what they have. He's a genius who knew exactly what he was doing. The foot wasn't an accident. That was part of his research.'

I feel sick.

He unlocks another door and beckons me through. I hear bubbling and splashing and taste salty air. In the dim light I make out three head-height glass tanks taking up the walls of the room. Dark shadows and bright flashes move everywhere. Tom takes a fishing net from behind the door, scoops something out of the nearest tank, and carries it to the tank at the far end of the room. I follow.

As my eyes become accustomed I see what looks like a human foot on the bottom of the tank. It is enlarged and viscousy but as I slowly make out toenails and an ankle I see that it is definitely human. I clench my teeth together and try to swallow the disgust pushing at my throat as I see, growing up from the enlarged ankle, several giant tentacles waving as they stun and trap in a split second the fish that Tom releases into the tank. The tentacles lower the fish into an opening in their centre.

'He started injecting himself with the anemone samples ten years ago. That's when he swelled up. Then he cut off bits of skin and ear, thinking if he could keep growing himself on from bits of his own body that he would never die, but when they didn't grow he intensified his treatment by injecting his brain, his heart, his groin. But he couldn't do it on his own. The injections were making him ill. So he cut off his foot and instructed me how to look after it – to make it survive on its own just like an anemone. And it worked – to a point... The rest of his body became a giant anemone and he began to drown in the air and his tentacles poisoned everything except his other foot. That foot found in his house won't survive in the hands of the scientists... But this one will.'

Co-creator
Rosemary Alves-Veira

Like humming birds
Scientific words
Fly from his brain
To the techno-terrain
Of manifest dreams,
Where themes of glory
And derring-do
Emerge with clout
From his mental brew:
Gene pool/cellular stew.

He claims his patents
Make life easier
Tho' some of us
Are getting wheezier.

But who could better
The vaulted blue,
Or majestic Earth,
Gem of the spiralling
Universe? Granting
Space for every
Life-form, breed and race.
Where man has made
His bed: And must lie in it too...

Why should we wish
To re-make the World?

But We Do
    We Do
        We Do!

Fox. Rabbit. Goose.
Rebecca Alexander

The gorgon is shrivelled, her body like a baby bird fallen from the nest, the skin red and wrinkled. Each breath in is an effort. Each breath out is a gasp. The mottled tissue paper that covers advancing bones is bruised in places, where she fell, where the ambulance men picked her up, where doctors probed for access to a threaded vein. Hilda is shrunken, a wraith. She drifts, her mind wandering in soundbites.

'I want to go home.'

When her eyes are open the whites are grey, the irises bleached blue. They glare at me and she presses her lips together.

'If I had a telly...but they won't let me have one.'

The television gleams, suspended over the bed on a skeletal arm. The room's blue and green colours wash onto it. The window squares a view over houses and the distant sea.

'They say it interferes with the drip.' Her eyes close again, her breathing fades. She's incontinent so she drains into a bag hung on the side of the bed. A trickle of orange is now the only sign she is alive.

A few minutes of sleep.

'I want to go home.' She rolls her eyes around the room. 'Have you just come from Ilfracombe?'

'No. We came down yesterday. I saw you, remember?'

'My daughter-in-law, she will be here soon.' Her eyes slide towards the light from the window, like a baby's, not really under her control. 'She doesn't approve of me smoking. And she's been all through my things.'

'I'm here.' She wanders again.

I have just driven two hundred miles. For this, I am missing my son's university interview.

*

May, 1990. It is Léonie who sleeps on the hospital sheets, meningitis fading slowly from her brain as the rash clears from her skin. She drifts from sleep into a waking dream of jungle print curtains and soft toys, children's nurses with brightly coloured uniforms. Hilda walks onto the ward, iron grey hair, grey polyester dress, flat shoes.

She ignores me, as I sit on the bed. The drips beep, chirping in a background of chimes and bells of monitors, of machines. Yellow antibiotic seeps into my four year old. The baby fusses in my arms; too hot, too tired in the eternal summer of Paediatric High Care.

Léonie opens her eyes at the sight of her grandmother.

'Nanny.' The words leak out of her through a fog of fever. 'I got Polie Bear.' She holds up the white bear, hand wavering, dropping onto the bed.

'Polar bear, polar,' Hilda says.

Léonie floats away again. I intervene. 'She's still sleepy, but she's better. She should be off the antibiotics tomorrow.'

Hilda drops statements without taking her eyes off the child. 'I made a book for her. It's of animals. We photographed the fox asleep in our garden, behind the pond. I put them in an album with the words. Lower case, like I said. Early readers need lower case.'

whatever.

Léonie rouses. 'Where's Grandpa?'

'Good. You're awake.' She smiles at Léonie, puts a carrier bag on her lap. 'I brought you a present.'

'Is it a video?' Léonie finally lifts her head to look at the bag.

'No. Look, it's to help you read.'

I smile at Léonie, trying to reassure her. 'She's only four. The pictures will be fine, for now.'

'With her disability she needs all the advantages she can get.' She presses her lips together, as if trying to hold back the outburst I have heard many times. *There's nothing like that in our family* Hilda opens the book.

'Look. Fox.' The picture is labelled underneath, Hilda tracing the word with a finger. 'F...o...ox. Fox. See?'

Léonie pulls at the corner of the card, to turn to the next page. Hilda resists. 'Can you say fox, Léonie?'

'Fox. It's Freda, she lives in your garden.'

'And rabbit. Can you say rabbit?' Léonie looks at me and yawns. She hugs her bear to her face. 'Rabbit. I'm tired. Show the baby.'

'And goose. Look, Léonie, a goose.'

'I don't like the goost.' She leans away from the page, perhaps remembering being pecked in a farm park we had visited the year before.

'Say goose.' Hilda is smiling, but firm.

Léonie frowns, suddenly reminding me of her grandmother. 'No. I don't like the goosts.'

I take the book from Léonie's hands, place it on the locker. 'I think she probably needs to sleep.'

Hilda turns to me, dropping her voice. 'It's such a shame she's like that. There's nothing like that on our side of the family, you know.'

The words drag me into the past, to the pregnancy with Léonie. Hilda had loomed over me then, shouting with her deep voice, strident with anger. 'There's nothing like that in our family. We'll get a solicitor and get you out of this house.' Her spittle had landed on my face, her mouth twisted.

'We're all very upset.' I had tried to be polite, trying to understand her disappointment through my own terror, grief, the baby moving under my hands. But underneath the patience, I was shocked, furious, hurt.

She had gone a deeper red and clenched her fists. I thought she was going to hit me. Go on, just one excuse to hit you back. She snatched her raincoat and her bag, turned in the doorway, and spat: 'I hope your baby dies.'

Yet, she loves Léonie, in her own way. The baby leans her hot head against my collarbone, finally tired. There is as much pity as anger, now. I pull back the blanket and curve the sleeping baby against her sister. As I lean over them, I smell starch, baby shampoo, plastic sheets.

It was a long time ago. The baby is grown up and at university. Léonie is dead. Only Hilda and I are left.

'I want to go home.' Her voice has lost its stridence.

I stand by her bed, stiff after hours in the car. 'You're dehydrated. Let the drip work.'

Her dry tongue looks like raw meat. It slowly licks her lips, searching first one corner, then the other.

'Would you like some water?'

She nods, and I put the glass in her clawed fingers, bent by arthritis and a lifetime of knitting. She is down to six stone. She takes one tiny sip, trembles the plastic beaker onto her tray.

'I had diarrhoea.'

I nod. There's nothing to say.

'I couldn't get to the bathroom.' She shuts her eyes again, drifts back into sleep. The sun stripes through vertical blinds, cutting her into strips. I'm afraid they are going to ask me to look after her.

Questions and statements float up but sleep claims her before I can answer.

'I wanted a television, but I couldn't have one... I want to go home and see Dotty... Did you just drive up from Ilfracombe?'

The doctor comes in and suddenly she's alert. 'When can I go home?'

He's looking at me, out of her eye line. 'I understand you had a fall, Hilda.'

'I only came in because my neighbour called an ambulance. I told her not to. But she was only trying to help.'

He opens the door and waves for me to follow. I smile at her, cover her blotchy feet with the blanket. The ward is buzzing with conversations by the nurses' station.

'And you are her daughter-in-law. I wondered if I might have a word with her son?'

'He died of leukaemia, nineteen years ago.' It seems a lifetime, the moment when he died and I didn't, the week when she cut me out of her will for surviving. She didn't speak to me for two years. 'I'm the next of kin.'

'I understand she has two brothers and a sister, all living nearby?'

'She fell out with them.' Thirty-odd years ago. They don't even exchange Christmas cards.

'She has food poisoning, and is very dehydrated. It's not surprising, if she isn't looking after herself properly.' His words feel like a rebuke.

'There's decaying food everywhere. Her kitchen is terrible. I cleaned it out when I got there this morning.'

The doctor is young, his skin deeply tanned, his dark eyes fringed with long lashes. He reminds me of my son, the one who is deciding his future at university today. I feel a pull, I wanted to be with him, to have the parents' tour and talk about finance and accommodation and meet his lecturers.

He bites his lip for a moment, looking away and lowering his voice. 'She also has an inflamed pancreas. I'm just warning you, it's very likely to be cancer. She either needs a lot of support from a care package or a residential home.'

I know she won't accept either.

Now, she is the body on the starched sheets. The words are social worker, care assistant, meals on wheels.

Dependence. Loneliness. Fear.

Our Late Friend
Rosemary Alves-Veira

All his life he had missed
opportunities, deadlines, buses, the
last post.

At his funeral they carried him every
inch of the way – 'You never know,'
they said.

Contributors' biographies

Gillian Kerr – having planned to be 'A Writer' all my life, it took the brilliant Writers' Groups at Barnstaple Library to kick-start me into action. The sky is now the limit! (Gillian working on polishing her novel. She also writes short stories and poetry).

Helen Robinson – I have explored the cutting edge of writing since age 6. I am a composer and piano teacher, linguist, artist, too creative to absorb facts or IT or admin.

Rosemary Alves-Veira – I am primarily a writer of short fiction, poetry and flash fiction, mostly inspired by Life's little surprises. I love change, movement, innovation and horses.

Sue Smith – is a recycled teenager with a passion for the Arts, including card craft, playing guitar and writing. She has developed her writing in local writing groups and has completed a ghost/mystery novel for NaNoWriMo. She was runner up in a local writing competition.

Chris Hodgson – I was born in Meddon Street, Bideford, a very short walk from the house where my father was born and my great-grandfather died. I grew up in exile in East the Water but still have recurring dreams about a particular property in Meddon Street – that I have never entered.

Aidan James – I am a young hopeful – I hope I can become a writer so I won't have to work! I enjoy video games and Japanese anime and manga, my writing being inspired by both of my hobbies.

Russell Bave – is a songwriter who has been a runner up in several UK Songwriter competitions and enjoys success both as a performer and writer.

Jessica McKinty – moved to North Devon with her family a couple of years ago. She has worked in non-fiction publishing and now works in distance learning education. She writes short stories and children's fiction and hopes to write a novel. This is her first publication.

Colin Z Smith was born and brought up in Essex, moving to Devon in 2000. An ex-insurance clerk, computer programmer, holiday-relief postman (for one week only) and freelance proofreader, he now cares for his disabled wife. He's loved writing since he first learned to hold a pencil, and has had stories and poems published in small-circulation magazines, The North Devon Journal and Devon Life. *Butterfly Dances*, included in this anthology, won second prize in the North Devon Biosphere B10 competition in 2013. The 'Z' is short for Zachary – for an explanation of that, see his website, www.colin-z-smith.com.

Mike Rigby. Born Sheffield 1937, moved to Hastings 1945. Joined the RAF in 1953 for twelve years as a wireless operator.
After demob, I was employed in electro-magnetics, and also with Pontins as an entertainer. In 1970 I joined the Civil Service and was medically retired in 1989. Interests: Music composition and playing guitar.

Nora Bendle is Devon born and bred, and has been writing short stories and poetry for many years. She has lived on a farm for more than 60 years. She belongs to a creative writing group in South Molton, and has been a member of other groups. She has performed readings for Amnesty International at Barnstaple Library.

Anne Beer. I first became fired up in creative writing 4 years ago when I belonged to a carers group, where each month a wonderfully encouraging lady came along and set us a subject to write about. The following month we would each read out to the group what we had written. I found this to be totally absorbing and satisfying, and now I can't stop! *My Grandmother's Kitchen* was one of the subjects set.

Diana Eilbeck. Born in Edinburgh, where I was educated at a girls' school before gaining an MA in Classics with English at Edinburgh University.Moved to England with my first husband, with whom I had two sons. Spent most of my working life as a teacher at both secondary and primary level, but also worked as a financial advisor for a while, and spent 4 years with HMRC after taking early retirement on health grounds from teaching. I now live quietly with my second husband (who has 4 sons) in our Devon cottage with a cat and a dog. We have frequent visits from friends and family, and I have two busy times of year when I do a lot of exam marking. Otherwise, I love watching/listening to cricket and tennis, doing crosswords and killer Sudoku, visiting my younger son in the US, and reading.

Maxine Osment Bracher – artist, illustrator, writer. LinkedIn and Facebook art page. email: maxinebracher@btinternet.com

Ruth Downie – is the author of six historical crime novels set in Roman Britain, published by Bloomsbury in the UK and US. In Ruth's words: 'Much of what Legionary medicus Ruso has been told about Britannia isn't true.' For more information visit Ruth's website at http://ruthdownie.com

Rebecca Alexander – is the author of three contemporary and historical fantasy novels published by Del Rey UK/Penguin Random House. Her novels have been placed in two major competitions, and she writes poetry. For more information visit http://www.rebecca-alexander.co.uk